I Will Survive

by

Larry Farmer

I Will Survive

Cover Art by *Debbie Taylor*

The Wild Rose Press, Inc.
PO Box 708
Adams Basin, NY 14410-0708
Visit us at www.thewildrosepress.com

Publishing History
First Vintage Rose Edition, 2020
Print ISBN 978-1-5092-3050-1
Digital ISBN 978-1-5092-3051-8

Published in the United States of America

"Elon," she said slowly and deliberately. "What kind of name is that? But never mind. I am not interested in your items from my friends in Hong Kong. I have a different agenda, if you don't mind me saying so. My Hong Kong friends said I would be interested in you. That you are tall, blond, and charming. Like a surfer boy from Los Angeles or something."

I felt the impact of a sneer oozing onto my face.

"I'm a farm boy from Texas," I corrected.

"Never mind that. You have well-defined muscles. I am indeed interested in you."

I studied her further, curious if I should be cautious or flattered.

"I am not so bold, Elon. Please hear my explanation. But come, please. Come out with me to the parking lot. I have a car. Be grateful. I am here to deliver you to your hostel where you will stay. Trust me. It will make sense."

I was indeed curious and somewhat flattered, too. I could handle this, I decided, as I walked with her toward the street and parking lots. I considered some triad trap somehow, or perhaps a prostitute ring, but none of that made sense. I had no money to be worthy of a ransom. Maybe I was worth beating up for being an American, now that Taiwan felt shunned by America. But even this consideration seemed paranoid.

Larry Farmer's Other Books

THE KERR CONSTRUCTION COMPANY
Dalhart McIlhenny, restless, searches for whatever it is he wants. But first he must find a job, one no one else wants, far away from fast cars and parties. Then he meets Carmen.

~*~

I WILL BE THE ONE
James and Lois each join the Peace Corps, while half a world away a political reformer is gunned down. Then Lois is threatened by the visit of a suspected spy to the remote village where she has been sent to teach.

~*~

SEEING GAIL AGAIN
Jericho returns from Vietnam only to face the anti-war movement. To avoid it, he finds peace in the Lake District of England—and a beautiful girl. Yet he abruptly leaves Gail to help Israel in the Yom Kippur War. Years later, can they resolve their feelings?

~*~

OVERLAND ON THE HIPPIE TRAIL
Hunter is not a hippie, but the open road lures him. In Vienna, a Polish girl, Ewa, gladly joins him on a trek to India. Shared experiences bond them, but the Cold War makes falling in love the worst hardship of all.

~*~

I WILL SURVIVE
Elon loves traveling the world, and curiosity leads him to Taiwan, though he's sick, broke, and unemployed. When he meets Brigitte, Belgian model and agent, he finds a fellow survivor who takes him under her wing.

Dedication

To my boyhood hero, Charlie Milstead

Chapter 1

Everyone back home in South Texas thought I would someday be a preacher. My name, Elon, even sounded like a preacher's name to some. The thought about being a preacher appealed, but I was the one person who knew I wouldn't be. I was too religious for that, in fact. I wanted answers. Real ones. Whatever those were. And being a preacher seemed too confining for all the answers I felt I needed. It was the search that was strong in me, not the call to a pulpit.

Part of the search focused on how I hated security. I seemed to thrive on being scared and coping with the unsureness of life. Somehow I sensed uncertainty kept me on my toes. Security also seemed too confining.

Trouble is, I hated insecurity too. It was nerve-wracking not having stability in my life. We're made for stability. It helps us heal and grow. The security issue was like a good workout. Like how one runs, or swims, or lifts weights. Workouts are strenuous and tear down the muscles. Then rest and nourishment are needed to rebuild, to grow stronger and more adept.

In time, it was traveling, more than religion, that held allure for the search in me. The spiritual search, I mean. There was always something going on while I backpacked around the world. Having a large frame helped the security part. All six foot three of me, with muscles. I had blond hair and blue eyes to match, as if some Viking figure. Having been in the Marine Corps helped the security angle some also. As if made to order, however, there was much insecurity in my bohemian life on the road, also, with all the unknowns in backpacking,

Each facet of my life after high school pushed me further out into the arena—the arena of life, you might say. Books, movies, or news accounts excited me—there was a world out there. The older I got and the farther from home, the more I wanted more of that world. Not just to picture it, but to face it. Encounter it.

I was a baby boomer of the sixties generation. I didn't care about hippies, but I did care about all the questions going on around me, which they seemed to represent. I was fascinated, not just by my questioning generation but by the ever-broadening scope of science and by the new cultures we mingled with in ever-widening circles, as well as by New Age thought.

So, after college, and after the Marines, I began to travel. Absolutely everything excited me as I did so, everywhere I went. When I arrived in Hong Kong, I wanted to stay. It was British and Chinese at the same time. A British colony set against Communist China. How intriguing!

Hong Kong was a beautiful city, from Victoria Island to the New Territories. I made my way through all of it, right up to the mainland Chinese border. Maybe I could teach English or something, so I hoped, but no, they had enough Brits for that.

I moved on. To Taiwan.

I first heard of Taiwan as Formosa. A Pacific island shaped like a tobacco leaf, between the Philippines and Japan, just off the coast of mainland

China. The Republic of China, it proudly called itself after Chairman Mao Zedong ran Chiang Kai-Shek off to it, along with a few other warlords. This last bastion of the Chinese old guard, tiny as it was, defied the Communist usurpers on the mainland. Chiang could be so bold knowing America would back him up if Chairman Mao, or his successor, sought to retake the island, as he swore to do someday. But now that I was on my way there, I was very unsure of my welcome. For things had changed politically. A great deal.

"I wouldn't do this if I were you," an American said to me while I waited for the bus to the airport in Hong Kong.

"It'll be okay," I assured him.

I had no idea if things were good in Taiwan or not. I just knew I was going anyway.

"Chiang's son doesn't have the same allegiance to America as his old man did," my American acquaintance said in a concerned tone. "When President Carter recognized the mainland at the beginning of this year as the true China, that left Taiwan not only unsure of their future but also bugged with us. So 1979 is a brand new year in a lot of ways, Elon. So much different from last year. I've heard some Taiwanese are threatening Americans now. Who knows, it may encourage the mainland to invade. Feeling we may accept them doing so, now that we see the mainland as the true China. We don't even have an embassy in Taipei anymore, you know."

"Yeah, but we have an attaché there," I countered. "A liaison. They still deal with passports if I need help. I think so, anyway. I'm ready to find out. I know Taiwan's bugged with us, but they still need us. I'll be okay."

The guy studied me. "Looks like you've made up your mind," he said easing into a supportive smile. "So, how's your cyst?"

"Cysts," I corrected. "Plural. They're getting worse. I still have bacteria from when I got infected in Thailand."

"I wouldn't let an infection go untreated," the guy advised.

"I've got some antibiotics left over from the doctor in Thailand," I said. "I saved some in case I had further problems. But they don't seem to be having an effect."

"What do you mean you 'saved' some? You don't save antibiotics. It'll spoil, most likely, in the tropical heat. Plus, they would have given you more than enough to get rid of that last germ. If you quit taking it too soon, and it sounds like you did, the germs are making a comeback and some of them may well now be immune to the antibiotics you've been taking. You never quit taking antibiotics, man. That's beginner stuff. You better see a doctor when you get to Taipei. As Taiwan's capital, they should have some good ones there. I hope they find another antidote for you. You don't mess with tropical germs, man."

I nodded that he was right and gave a frustrated huff.

"Some are abscessed now," I mentioned, showing some of my nervousness. "Little boils and cones have been popping up all over me, but also one on each buttock. I sat on those, and they abscessed. No release of pus from them. The cones just keep growing there, and the pus oozes out through the pores."

"Listen, Elon, you're scaring me. I'm telling you—

first thing after you arrive, you go see a doctor. Promise me this."

"I don't have money for a doctor," I replied.

"You don't have money to be sick half way around the world and unemployed. Promise me, man. Do you hear?"

I looked back at him to promise, but I knew I wasn't going to see a doctor.

Chapter 2

Where would fate take me now? I wondered as my plane descended to Taipei. I was nervous, but comfortable with the insecurity I seemed to crave. Here I was in another foreign country and coping with a language I could never hope to understand, in a country at odds with one of our worst enemies but now superseded by that enemy as the legitimate China—a former ally no longer recognized.

I was in a very vulnerable setting.

At customs, the agent studied the contents of my backpack. Soon, he looked at me cynically. I expected as much and was ready for him.

"Where are the receipts for these items?" he asked with a bite.

"Which items are you talking about?" I asked incredulously.

But I knew exactly the ones that concerned him.

"For this cassette player," he answered. "For the radio and camera. What do you mean to do with these items?"

"I brought them with me from America," I lied. "You know, I'm a tourist. I want to take some pictures as I travel."

"And the radio and cassette player," he harped.

"To listen to the local stations and to play music," I answered.

"Where are your tapes if you want to play music?"

I went to a side pocket of the backpack and pulled out a single cassette tape. It was one I kept for recording melodies that popped into my head at times. To add to the ruse, I pulled out a few pictures of Bangkok someone had given me there, as if I had taken them myself with this camera.

He was far from convinced, but he waved me on through customs.

I made it. The first of many obstacles down.

None of the items I was smuggling were expensive, but expensive enough it was worth it to the dealer back in Hong Kong to risk sneaking them into Taiwan for a profit. I didn't know why this black market vendor thought he could trust me, but he did. He played the odds enough to know the risks, I decided.

Now to collect my reward for getting these items into Taiwan—a free night at a hostel in Taipei. It wasn't just the free night that interested me. It meant I had an address and didn't have to look for a place to stay. A place that meant contacts with other Westerners.

As I made my way through the lobby of the airport toward the street, I noticed an attractive-looking white girl. She was strawberry-blonde, tall for a girl, and looked to be in her twenties. She intensely scoped out the departing passengers. Her focus landed occasionally on me before she checked out other passengers again. She held up a sign saying BRIGITTE.

"Excuse me," I heard her call out finally in what resembled a French accent. "Are you Allen? Is your name Allen?"

She was addressing me.

"My name is Elon," I said politely as I approached

her.

"Elon, long e," she said with emphasis. "A long e American sound, not a for Allen. Accent on the first syllable." She shook her head in frustration. "*Merde*," she cursed in French, "so much gets lost in translation."

"You were looking for someone?" I asked quizzically.

"Did you just come from Hong Kong?" she inquired further. "And are on your way to a free night at a hostel near here?"

I studied her.

"It's all right," she continued. "I was supposed to meet you here. You didn't know?"

I shook my head as I kept my focus on her.

"Nothing's wrong," she said with a warm smile. "I am not from the gestapo. But I have contacts in Hong Kong. Nothing concerning your free night at the hostel here. But many pass through Taiwan from Hong Kong for my friends there. I assume you know the ones I'm talking about. They gave you some items to deliver." Her smile broadened. "I'm really not scrutinizing you. Isn't that the word? To scrutinize, to make sense of something or someone?"

She held out her hand to shake mine.

"I am Brigitte," she said as she did so. "From Belgium. So a French sound of Brigitte, while we analyze names. Accent on the second syllable with a soft g sound followed by an i sounding like e in American English. Not Bridgette, like the name Gidget, but Brigitte."

I shook her hand in return while I smiled back at her.

"Elon," she said slowly and deliberately. "What

kind of name is that? But never mind. I am not interested in your items from my friends in Hong Kong. I have a different agenda, if you don't mind me saying so. My Hong Kong friends said I would be interested in you. That you are tall, blond, and charming. Like a surfer boy from Los Angeles or something."

I felt the impact of a sneer oozing onto my face.

"I'm a farm boy from Texas," I corrected.

"Never mind that. You have well-defined muscles. I am indeed interested in you."

I studied her further, curious if I should be cautious or flattered.

"I am not so bold, Elon. Please hear my explanation. But come, please. Come out with me to the parking lot. I have a car. Be grateful. I am here to deliver you to your hostel where you will stay. Trust me. It will make sense."

I was indeed curious and somewhat flattered, too. I could handle this, I decided, as I walked with her toward the street and parking lots. I considered some triad trap somehow, or perhaps a prostitute ring, but none of that made sense. I had no money to be worthy of a ransom. Maybe I was worth beating up for being an American, now that Taiwan felt shunned by America. But even this consideration seemed paranoid.

"I am the head of a modeling agency here in Taipei," she explained as we walked. "I am originally from Belgium, as I said already, a small town there, Braine-l'Alleud, near Waterloo. You know of Napoleon in history? How he met his Waterloo? Waterloo is rather near Brussels. But three years ago I found work as a model here, and we were quite compatible together, this agency and myself. There are so many

Westerners passing through here. We need mostly Chinese models, but there is also sometimes a call for Westerners—European or American, makes no difference. My friends in Hong Kong said I would be interested in you. Could you help us, Elon? You would have to get a working visa, though. Would that be agreeable to you? I can help you with that. Can you consider this proposition that I make?"

I flinched as I heard the details. This was too easy. I wasn't used to easy. It interested me, but what does one do with such luck? Somehow, something was up.

"Am I too much for you now, Elon?" she asked with a laugh. "My friends in Hong Kong were supposed to tell you about me. But perhaps you would have been leery and not delivered the items of theirs. They told me you wanted to teach English here. That you needed money. I don't know what all you told them. We talked on the telephone this morning. They call me up when there is a prospect. This prospect was you this time. I know they asked you questions about your itinerary here. They often need such as you to smuggle electronic devices to Taiwan. So they ask questions many times. They told me some of this. I don't mean to make you nervous."

"No, so far you're right on," I answered, beginning to ease up around her. "All this you're saying does interest me. I do need a job and a visa. Yes, you were coming at me pretty hard with all this, and I wasn't expecting it. I'm interested in learning more from you."

As we walked out into the street toward the parking lot where her car was parked, someone called out.

"Are you American?" a husky female voice behind me asked.

I turned to see. A short, chubby, elderly Caucasian woman sneered my way. Her red hair was speckled with gray. She seemed angry.

"I need help, if you don't mind," she informed. "Someone from back home who is big and strong like you."

I walked back toward her.

"I have all these bags," she continued. "Suitcases, you know. They are bulky and heavy. I need to get my car from the parking lot where you were headed. Can you watch my luggage for me while I do this? It will only be a minute until I get my car. I live here in Taipei. My husband is busy and couldn't pick me up, but he left a car for me. I cannot possibly handle loading all these suitcases—if you don't mind. I just flew in from seeing my daughter in Los Angeles. My husband works for the attaché's office of the US consulate here. It used to be the US Embassy, but you know what happened. Carter and all. Recognizing mainland China and all."

"Sure," I replied. "I can help you with your luggage."

I then looked at Brigitte to see if she approved. She smiled and followed me to the curb next to the lady's baggage.

Our total train of thought seemed gone now, concerning our conversation about me working in Taiwan, including as a model. But, as the lady promised, within minutes she pulled up in her car and parked by the curb to load up.

She seemed impatient and ill at ease as I handled her suitcases for her. When I finished, I closed her car trunk and proceeded to the parking lot with Brigitte.

"Wait, young man," the lady called out.

She opened her purse and pulled out a money pouch.

"For your effort," she said, shoving several bills of Taiwan currency at me.

She waited for me to take them.

I shook my head no, that I didn't want her money. She pushed her hand with the bills at me once again. I again shook my head. The lady grimaced, then pushed the money at Brigitte.

"I have to go," the lady said after forcing the bills into Brigitte's hand.

She got back into her car and departed.

"I would rather have a 'thank you' than money," I said with a bite in my voice. "I feel like a bellboy."

"Why didn't you take the money?" Brigitte asked me curiously. "You're broke. This was your first job, Elon. Sort of."

"People where I'm from don't take money for helping people in need," I said emphatically. "It insulted me. I felt degraded. I could have handled it if she hadn't been so gruff and demanding. Then she shoved the money at me like I was a coolie."

Brigitte motioned for us to continue to her car. She seemed humored by the event. We walked on while she folded the bills and placed them inside her pants pocket.

"We are here, Elon," she said as she bent over to unlock the passenger side of her small car to let me in. "Let us talk more on the way. Back to the real world. Our real world here in Taiwan. I will explain our situation. Yours and mine. Get in. We'll talk on the way."

She proceeded to get into the driver's seat.

"I have a network of sorts now, about these

things," she continued as we drove along. "How to get things done here to survive, I mean. I know my way, you might say. We will check you into your hostel first. They can help you find work as an English instructor in one of the many private language schools here. These schools know to look for native English speakers at a hostel like where we are going. But to do so, you must have a work visa. That's easy."

Her mind turned to the heavy traffic we now were encountering. Once established in a steady lane, she turned to me to continue our talk.

"It is over half an hour's drive to the hostel," she informed. "Depending on the traffic. There are two national universities here, even more, actually, but two in particular that take foreign tourists as students, to teach them Mandarin. To enroll makes you officially a college student and eligible for a student visa, which allows you to work legally here. I will be with you as we talk to management at the hostel. They have all the contacts and are experienced. It is good business for them to know these things. People like you choose there to stay for such help. I know the ropes also. Isn't that an American saying? To know the ropes. I can help you. With a motive. I hope you will work for me as a model."

She looked over at me with a wide grin.

"What do you think, my dear?" she asked.

"You're quite an entrepreneur," I replied.

"That is quite a nice French word, is it not?" she said with a warm smile. "Entrepreneur. Brigitte and entrepreneur are very nice French names, yes?"

She winked.

I melted. I adored her already.

"Elon, I have lived here for three years now, as I said. Let me tell you something. The contrast here you will see leaves no doubt. No theory, as in Europe. Here it is in your face. There is Hong Kong, and there is the Republic of China, Taiwan, you know. And there is the People's Republic of China—or mainland China, as we call it. The contrasts between the mainland and here are in your face. Another American saying that I like. In your face. Americans are so clever with their words. In your face. It is in your face here, Elon. Hong Kong is a colony, Taiwan a developing country. Both have a poor population, but with hope and promise and the spirit of the entrepreneur. There is no such entrepreneurial element on the mainland. I have no idea of your political ideas. Forget theory while you are here, Elon, no matter what your politics. You can make it here, even as you struggle. Live, Elon. Breathe the air, smoggy air that it is. Breathe it. We will thrive here, Elon, you and me, even as we struggle."

Chapter 3

"This is Elon," Brigitte introduced me to the young clerk behind the counter of the hostel. "He just came from Hong Kong."

The clerk scoped me out before easing into a smile, then turned back to Brigitte to speak.

"He is expecting a free night with us?" the clerk asked with a heavy Chinese accent.

Brigitte nodded her head yes as a reply. She then turned toward me.

"You can give your items to him," she instructed. "Then he'll show you to your room. I should say a squadbay, actually. I hope you weren't expecting more."

"It's what I'm used to," I answered her. "Or less."

"Are you okay for now?" she asked me. "Can I check on you later? Would tonight be too sudden for you or would you like to get your bearings? You will probably want to check about a Mandarin course. I would do that first thing. You will need this visa it gets you if you want to work for me legally and to teach at a language school. Our friend here can direct you, but you will meet others in the hostel that know things. I can help also if you need, but I doubt you need me for any of this. This hostel is a wealth of information to get started. But I'd like to see you again, nevertheless, to check on your status and needs. And to follow through with you that I indeed hope to hire you as a model for my agency."

"I'd like to see you again," I assured her. "You're my first friend here. You've been very kind and helpful."

"Yes then, so let us meet tonight," she offered warmly. "I am happy here, but also to have some Western friends is a treat for me. Plus, if I may say so, since you are a prospect for me as a model, also for practical reasons. There will be movie scouts here now and then also, to see who may appear in a Taiwanese movie. I am sure you will be offered something. I know movie agents also. I can introduce you. You won't be so well off in spite of how it may sound. I hope this doesn't sound like some elaborate setup. It is in part, but again this is a small developing country. You will need everything you can get just to survive, or hopefully have a bit extra. I have been here for three years, as I said. I am happy and am making it quite well. But I had to be an entrepreneur. I learned the ropes."

She grinned my way.

"How do you like my American way to talk? I love English. Anyway, ciao, my friend. See you tonight. Around six. I will meet you here at this desk."

I was already so used to Brigitte handling everything for me, I suddenly became disoriented with her gone. My tasks were minimal, but now it was left to me to do them.

"Brigitte mentioned I could take a Mandarin course while I'm here," I mentioned to the clerk at the hostel.

"Yes," he replied. "There are two universities here that give student visas to study. First, find a locker near your bed and put up your belongings. Come back and I will give you the names of these universities."

I nodded approval, then walked on into the main portion of the hostel, which was a squadbay of bunk beds. I found a top bunk near the window looking out into the streets below. We were on the second floor of the building. I was glad we weren't on a higher floor, since I was scared of heights.

I put my backpack into a metal locker near my bunk after unpacking it. I had a combination lock from my days in Sri Lanka; I'd bought it after my camera was stolen at a small hostel near Adams Peak. An inexpensive camera, but with its theft, I had no way of taking pictures. A camera was one of the first things I hoped to buy once I found a job.

"Both universities are near the hostel," the clerk explained to me upon my return from unloading my gear. "They are inexpensive. The Mandarin classes are small."

It was a coin toss in my mind as to which university to use. I loved my days in college and was delighted at the thought of being around one again, limited as my time there would probably be.

"Classes begin tomorrow," the lady told me at the university I chose. I wasn't sure if she was a clerk, a secretary, or administrative staff. But she took my money for the fee and gave me the classroom number and building site. "There are three of you now," she informed. "As soon as we have three students we begin a class. You make the third, so a class is formed with you. It begins tomorrow morning at nine."

Just like that. The ease of success gave me confidence. I was grateful for how smoothly everything had gone up to now.

"Very good," the clerk at the hostel said to me when I told him I would have a student visa by the next day. "There are many English language schools wanting to hire Americans. The need is so great they take Europeans if their English is good. A college degree of any kind is required, but they seldom ask to see. They just want someone who speaks good English."

As if on cue, a man walked into the hostel.

"Good morning, Mr. Chu," the hostel clerk said to him in English. "I put up your notice for English instructors on our bulletin board. By coincidence, here is an American with a university degree right here." The clerk looked at me. "His name is Elon. He was just inquiring about being an English instructor as you arrived, Mr. Chu. He will have a student working visa by tomorrow."

This man, Mr. Chu, sent a broad, warm smile my way.

"If you have not found a school to work at, please consider me," he said.

"I haven't found one," I said with renewed optimism. "I was going to check out some now, as a matter of fact. You're looking for another teacher?"

"Very much so," he replied, holding out his hand for me to shake. "We are a new school, and there is big demand from prospective students. We very much need instructors."

"I would love to teach at your school," I said happily.

"If you get your working visa tomorrow, when could you begin with us?" he asked.

"Tomorrow afternoon, I suppose. I'll bring my visa to you as soon as I get it."

"How many hours are you available for us?" Mr. Chu asked.

"Forty," I answered. "Even more."

"That's very encouraging, but I can tell you have never been an instructor before. It sounds simple, and it is, for the most part, but very demanding and will exhaust you soon. We recommend only twenty. Twenty will be all you will want."

I let my disappointment show. I needed money. And though there was a big demand for instructors, the pay was not good, as Brigitte had warned me. Students were not rich. In fact, the biggest reason most wanted to know English was in the hope of getting to America, either with some job or as a student. They did not make much money in Taiwan.

"I'm yours," I told him. "When do I start?"

"I am sure we can begin with you by tomorrow afternoon."

He reached into his back pocket to retrieve his wallet.

"Take my business card," he instructed as he handed it to me. "Come see me in an hour. By then I will have your schedule. My school is a short walk from here and easy to find. Just ask anyone here or on the streets for this address. I am looking forward to working with you."

Brigitte came to mind. I had a job with her too. Whatever that meant. How often I would be needed to model I hadn't a clue. But it all provided the confidence I needed.

"Brigitte," I said on the phone from the hostel,

which the clerk there let me use.

"Is this Elon?" she asked surprised. "How did you get my number? From the hostel? I was coming to see you tonight. Remember?"

"Yes, I could have waited until then, but I was anxious to tell you. It was easy, like you said, to get a student work visa. I'll have it by tomorrow. And I've been hired for twenty hours a week at an English school. But I'll barely survive on that. So, for the record—officially, you know—I am interested in working for you as a model or whatever you've got."

"I need models, male and American, meaning you. So we can get things rolling tonight by discussing what you should expect. It is good to have you on board, Elon."

"Good to be in your stable," I replied. "Isn't that what we are, your stable?"

"I have heard it called that," she said with a chuckle. "And worse. I must train you, but it is easy. We will start tomorrow, in fact, with the training. We have a show next week at a large department store. I can get you ready by then. You don't get paid for the training, only the shows. Are you still game? Is that how you say it? I love having an American to talk to regularly now. I heard that, 'are you still game,' from American TV shows here."

"I am game," I answered. "So do we still need to meet tonight?"

"It wouldn't hurt," she replied. "Plus, let's get to know one another. How about meeting at your favorite restaurant? How's that for cozy and casual?"

"I don't have a favorite restaurant yet," I answered her. "And I don't have money yet for a favorite restaurant."

"So you will just starve until you get paid? Or what, *mon cheri*?"

Her term of endearment sent chills down my spine.

"It's just a hint of my condition," I said. "Can we meet at a greasy spoon? I have money for that."

"Ew, Elon. What, pray tell, is a greasy spoon? It sounds—I am not sure of the English to use for how it sounds. What is a greasy spoon, and perhaps I can think of a word for it."

"A cheap place," I explained. "I love Chinese food, so I'll be easy to please. But let's find one that's a mom-and-pop joint. Cheap. For the masses. Soon, because of me, you'll know many more American slang phrases. I'm valuable to you. Remember that."

"I love these American slang words you use, Elon. Yes, we will find a place you can afford. Mom-and-pop as you said. I will pay. That is even cheaper for you. I will use the money you refused from the American lady at the airport. Remember her? So, alas, you will pay for mine also with that money that is now mine. Thank you, Elon, my new client."

I knew not to get carried away, but the meeting with her now felt like a date. I liked the feeling and decided to go with it.

We didn't use her car but found a place within a short walk of the hostel. Going by the looks, it indeed was the kind of place I was looking for—working-class people eating simple meals. I assumed cheap meals. It had a buffet-type serving, with many dishes displayed from a long counter. People paid and helped themselves. If this was cheap, and they served food like this, Taiwan was paradise. Wonton soup, plain rice, fried rice, mixed vegetables, chicken, pork, beef strips, and fish, all cooked simply and put out for us.

"You seem satisfied with your meal," Brigitte said to me while we ate at a table that was clean but with scratches on the top and carvings at the legs.

"I'll go to a fancy place someday," I replied, "but I could eat here forever."

"Yes, the food is very good all over the city. All over the island, actually. Have you seen the food carts on the sides of the streets? Even they are wonderful. Boiled eggs soaked in soy. Fried onions. Pork legs. Even chicken claws, but I don't care so much for that."

I chuckled at the grotesque thought of a chicken claw.

"And I can live without the octopus tentacles, with all their suckers," I added.

"But so much selection is the marvel," Brigitte said. "Everywhere you look, there are so many choices. So forget the local items that make you gag. Another good American word. Gag. I love that word for the food items that taunt our sanity."

"I don't know what they do to it here," I said approvingly, "but the food tastes so Chinese. That's the test. Does it taste Chinese?"

"That's why I brought you here," she said. "I have not been to this particular establishment, but there are so many like this, and this one is near you."

I looked at her, wondering if I should ask what was on my mind.

"Have you taken out many Americans?" I quizzed her.

She smirked as she studied me.

"I occasionally go out with my clients or

employees," she replied. "But usually after I get to know them. After we have worked together a bit. Why did you ask such a question? I guess it is not the question but the way you asked it. As if you really want to know, my dear fellow."

"Yeah," I replied. "Yeah. I want to know this. Is that okay with you? Why isn't someone like you going with someone regularly, after living here three years?"

"Someone like me?" she asked with a tease. "Just who is someone like me? You began this direction of conversation. Please add some depth to it."

"You're established here. You do well. And you're so pretty."

"You consider me pretty?"

"You know the answer to that. You know you're pretty. So let's get to it. Why aren't you going with someone?"

"And how did you determine that I am not going with someone?"

Her bluntness stung. I still believed she wasn't going with anyone, but she was right. Just how did I decide such a thing?

"Is this a trait you have, Elon? This directness? Is it so important to you to know this?"

"I'm more than curious."

"I have not time for relationships," she answered, to the point. "This is not my country, nor my culture. It is a small developing country half way around the world from my home. Even the Westerners do not interest me. Including the men. I have no time for such things. I am just passing through. I do not want such relationships. I do not want to worry about such things. I enjoy my time here, and I have a job to do. When I go home to Belgium, whenever that happens, I will be ready. But for now, I have things to do and to experience and to see where it leads me."

She pursed her lips and looked me directly in the eyes without blinking.

"Does that answer you, Elon? Is it good I am this way? Are you interested in me, Elon? What would you do with such as me in my circumstances? I think you are an adventurer and women are part of the adventure. I am flattered, but I have no interest."

Should I get bolder? I asked myself.

"You seem attracted to me," I said bluntly, flirting a little.

She blurted out a laugh.

"You are indeed interesting, my dear man. And I admit, also attractive."

She seemed ready to say something more, then took another bite from her plate instead.

Another adventure for me had indeed begun. I hoped it had for her also.

Chapter 4

Everyone knew some English in these classes at Mr. Chu's school before they entered. They were set on improving their skills. That made my job easier.

I was already amazed from my days in Europe, where it seemed three-fourths of the continent spoke English as a second language—plus, quite often, other languages as well. It put my American upbringing to shame. I wasn't even good at Spanish, in spite of growing up on the border with Mexico. Now I witnessed the Taiwanese speaking English so well.

"*You mean he took all the dishes,*" the man read out loud in class. "*That's incredible,*" he read further.

The reader paused to look up at me.

"I thought 'incredible' was a positive word," he said. "Like something very good. But stealing is a bad thing and it is being called incredible. I do not understand."

So this proved to be my English lesson for the day also. I had to think about the point he just raised. One I had always taken for granted. I supposed this was why Mr. Chu wanted teachers with a college education. Easy questions aren't always easily answered, and the school wanted an academic background from the teacher.

"You're right," I replied. "Incredible is like a big positive exclamation. But it is used with some sarcasm here. Do you know what I mean by sarcasm?"

"Irony or satire," the man replied.

I was impressed he knew these words. I began to wonder why I was surprised.

"Yes," I said. "There is a bit of irony in the way 'incredible' is used here. It is still denoting a big expression of emotion or amazement. But in a satirical way."

"I don't understand," the man quizzed further.

I had to think again.

"Because the one using the word 'incredible' is baffled in a negative way about it. The thief took all the dishes. Every last one of them. And they were his dishes, belonging to the man using the word. He needed a big word to express his feelings. Even bigger than big. So the need for big overcame the positive use. Big negative instead. Baffled, angry."

The man wasn't convinced but left it.

Challenges like this at least spiced up the lessons. But they also tired me further. I was glad now I only taught twenty hours a week.

I had other encounters in class, also. I was a single American male. One woman attended classes with her daughter. She did so to let me know she was Christian and that her daughter was available. Very available. She hoped I would be interested in both aspects.

I didn't really want or expect celibacy during my stay in Taiwan, but I was very reluctant to indulge in a relationship. Somehow, it wasn't going to be a simple, nice, innocent endeavor if I did so. I thought of my conversation with Brigitte about relationships. I could appreciate her attitude of avoiding romantic flirtations and directions. If something came about, she would be careful, but it would be better to avoid.

There was one woman even more blatant.

"I do not care to read," the woman told me.

She was in her early twenties and very pretty, the prettiest of any of my students. She paid extra to be the only student in this particular class. She was well off as the daughter of a rich industrialist. She even owned, at such a young age, her own car, a new one at that.

"Can we just converse?" she asked.

"We really need to read," I said in a pushy manner. "There are words and imagery that are presented in the stories that will help you expand your vocabulary."

"Never mind this," she answered. "I do not want to study or work in America. I want to marry an American. To be able to talk with my husband and friends there."

"Oh, you're getting married?" I asked.

"Not yet. I'm looking for an American I would want to marry."

That pronouncement left me nervous and speechless.

I regrouped.

"We can try without reading, I guess," I replied.

"My name is Yuanjing. English name for me is then Jean. Please call me Jean while we converse. You are Elon."

I nodded that was my name.

"So you are from this place called Texas?" she asked me.

"Yes," I answered.

"I like Texas," she commented. "There are so many movies about Texas. I would like to live in Texas, I think."

"It's a big place," I replied. "Many places there are

27

very different from here and very different from what you see in movies. You may not like where you live in Texas if you go there."

"Then we could move. Why have you not been married?"

"I don't have time for that," I answered. "I went to college, then joined the Marines, then traveled around."

"The Marines are so impressive," she commented.

"I enjoyed it."

"I would love to travel around. That sounds very nice. I like educated men, too. You seem very interesting. I am surprised you are not married."

I was not only taken aback by her forwardness, but it also worried me. What would her father think about her running off with someone like me if I was interested? Or some aspiring suitor here who saw a fortune in marrying her? She seemed like trouble.

"I don't want to teach this girl," I told Mr. Chu after my class with the rich girl, Jean. "She didn't want to read from the book. Just talk."

That was the best excuse I could think of to tell him.

"She is a very important client," he told me. "She pays well and is dependable. She was with another teacher but seems to want to learn from you. I would take it as a favor if you would teach her."

"I don't feel good around her. She seems to want to take charge of the class. I'm not sure how much I can accomplish with her."

Mr. Chu shrugged and gave a sigh.

"As you wish," he said, but his face showed his disappointment.

At least the trainings with Brigitte were fun. Not

really, but being with Brigitte definitely was.

"Our first show with you is here at this department store," she reminded me after a practice run. "You seem to have it down well enough. Are you enjoying it so far?"

"I'm a little embarrassed to wear pajamas," I answered her.

"That's just for one segment," she said with a laugh. "We had to search to find a pair big enough for you. That is true for all our fashions, actually, but especially the pajamas. We managed since this is a big department store. They had some your size, yet not really what we wanted to display. It will work out fine. But, Elon…"

Her demeanor suddenly turned serious.

"Your sores are getting bigger and more of them. They may even damage the clothes you model for us. I know you are wearing Band-Aids to protect the clothing, but it is a concern if there is leakage. We cannot have that. I worry about you, also. You said the antibiotics you take do not help?"

"I'm out of them."

"You get paid tomorrow after the show. You need to see a doctor."

I instinctively was ready to argue with her but hesitated. My condition was indeed worse. I was beginning to worry. Pus was still oozing out of two of the sores, and another couple were bleeding. The ones that were exposed outside the clothes could be partially hidden with a lotion but were still apparent.

I nodded my head toward Brigitte that I would indeed go see a doctor.

"I may wait until I get paid by the school," I said.

"The money tomorrow from you will pay another week at the hostel and give me some money to live on until I get paid again for my English lessons."

"Are you so terribly poor, my dear Elon? You are beginning to sound pathetic. Would you like me to advance you some money? You really need to see a doctor."

"I'm okay," I replied bravely.

By now, however, I didn't feel brave anymore at all. More like foolish. Surely, it was a good sign that I felt this way. A step up. I wasn't sure if my carelessness about seeing a doctor was left over from my days in the field with the Marines, or from all the traveling I had done. Now it was getting through to me that I was carrying it all too far. I would have avoided seeing a doctor in Thailand also if not for the huge cone on my left forearm that began gushing pus, as well as the fever that accompanied it. But once the pus and fever were gone after the initial dose of antibiotics I took, I was back to feeling brave. Maybe it was the Texan in me. Doctors just seemed to be for wimps, in my psyche.

"Let's have a beer, Elon," Brigitte said, to change the mood.

"Sure."

We usually had a beer after rehearsals. It was automatic now.

We walked to a tavern near the department store, one we had grown to favor. This one had a singer with a guitar. He sang mostly in English, but with a strong Chinese accent. It wasn't just his accent, however, that attracted our attention, but the way he pronounced certain words. Though his voice was pleasant, it took adjusting to his Chinese presentation of American

I Will Survive

songs before it quit sounding comical to us. Now we were at the point of enjoying his performance, even because of his accent.

"You will do fine tomorrow," Brigitte said as we sipped on our beer while we listened to the singer. "You have it down. It's easy enough, but you have it down. Like packed down, I guess."

"You seem so curious about English," I said approvingly to her. "Not just the language itself, but the idioms and mindsets."

"It helps me learn the language," she explained. "English rules the world. I know Flemish, Dutch, German, French, and now a bit of Mandarin Chinese, I suppose. But English opens doors like no other. You have to know more than the words—you have to be American while you speak it. So I key in. Luckily, I keep running across Americans or watch American TV. I did in Belgium, but more so here. In Belgium my own language was a distraction. It is what we spoke and how we got by. But here, it is English, in particular American English, not so much the British English. So no distractions in my English education now."

"Are they so different?" I asked. "American versus British English?"

"For the most part no, but that's oversimplifying. There are special words Europeans, British, you know, use, and certain special American words. I'm glad of my curiosity about it because it helps me focus. I find it intriguing. But also there are phrases and ways to put things that a Brit says differently than an American. Canadians are a bit of both, but mostly American. Anyway, I feel I need to know this for my job. Not so much here, but what if I want to carry being a model further. Like go to Hollywood."

"So you do think about your future," I noted. I wasn't sure why that surprised me. "I assumed you must, at least some, but you never show a sign of it." I shrugged. "I'm only just getting to know you, though."

"Oh, yes," she said with a pronounced sigh. "I am very thoughtful about my future. I am twenty-five. That sounds young, but to be a model, a girl, I better get moving. I have a good place here, so I am happy. But for how long? I must make a move soon, or be stuck here. Or go back perhaps to our family farm in Belgium."

"Farm?" I asked perking up as I studied her. "You don't look like a farm girl."

"No? I don't? And pray tell, how does a farm girl look, *Monsieur* Elon?"

She called me the French name for Mister. Even as old hat as that word was used in the English language at times, her saying it melted me. She was French. Belgian French, anyway. It made me feel like her pet.

"Farm girls are often pretty, but seldom like a model," I replied. "So I supposed."

"Perhaps I should have big muscles, my friend. I don't know how one should look, only that I am a farm girl from Belgium, now living as a model in Taiwan."

"I grew up on a farm in Texas," I told her.

She smiled at that.

"I can see this," she said. "Big and strong. But you are not rugged in the face."

"So, if you don't find your future soon," I mused further, "you may end up back on the farm? Like sink or swim."

"Yes, sink or swim. Another Americanism saying.

It would not be so punishing to go back. I enjoyed the farm growing up. But I don't want to be tied to a farm. Or anything. I suppose even being a model is being tied down. But I'm thinking it could lead to other prospects. Something will tie me. By then I will be ready. A model is old and out of date very quickly. So, I must learn something else. That is why I am still here. I run the agency. Like a manager anyway, not necessarily like an owner, though it's close enough at times. That is a skill. Besides being a model, the product you might say, I know how to be a manager. That is a start for broadening my scope."

"Except farming is a business also," I added. "You must manage and own the farm. It's a science, even."

"Yes, this is true. But somehow I feel stuck when I think of our farm."

"Why would you go back to the farm, then? You don't have a brother?"

"A younger sister. We can be the manager, but there is so much physical labor to a farm, so it helps to have a man. We can always hire a man. Or marry a man. I don't know, Elon. How did we get on this conversation? Oh yes, our future. My future, I mean. Now is the time to seek my future. I am here and seeking. The farm is not a threat to me, but I want to have options. That is the deal, I suppose. Options in my life. I want options while I have the chance. For now I am here, and for now I have a sister that can take over our farm someday, so that I don't have to make a decision now."

I nodded that I understood.

"And you, Elon? Speaking of futures, do you have one in mind for you?"

"Somewhere out there," I returned.

"Somewhere out there," she repeated. "You seem in no hurry. Ha."

"When you struggle in quicksand you only sink farther," I came back.

She let out a laugh at my reply.

"Quicksand, you say. You are in quicksand."

"I was brought up to worry about my future," I began my explanation. "I understand why I should. I took things very seriously when I was growing up. And then my generation, our generation, got on drugs, sex, and rock and roll. Partying. Don't corrupt or pollute life with capitalism. Or whatever. Make love not war. I have to admit I didn't know much, growing up. I did know one thing, though. I didn't like our generation. Too many scoff at traditions and the old ways. Just when I considered they were thinkers, they traded the old set of rules for new ones. Little more than that. A bit of depth at times, but mostly lacking. Mostly just a new set of rules. It was like an either/or situation. No real depth. So I was on my own then to create any depth. No real direction except what I could make on my own. My generation did get it through to me how I didn't know anything. So for that I am grateful. And here I am. Still looking."

"Some of our generation traded our values for Chairman Mao's Little Red Book," she reinforced.

"Exactly," I concurred.

"So you are a hippie or not, then? You live like one, except for no drugs, sex, or rock and roll, I suppose. And by your explanation just now you hate our generation. You have no beard and have short blond hair. This complex person I am with, and his walking contradictions."

"I don't know." I sighed. "I don't feel like a hippie. Do they still exist? Did they ever? But yes, I live like one. And for sure without the drugs, sex, and rock and roll."

"So you are not a hippie. Then why are you here? To be a model?"

"Answers," I replied. "Better yet, for the questions that appear while I look for answers. I need to breathe, to think. To live and experience. I'm sure I'll settle down. But I don't know when."

"Are you so sure you will settle down? You seem lost, to me. Seeking answers, you say. You do sound confused, but I think you just don't want to settle down."

"For lack of a better explanation, 'lost' will do. But I do need answers. I seem irresponsible to you, I know, but I can tell you, things churn inside me and I can't live with myself. I even need the questioning I do. Huge. Life makes me think. Our generation does. Even having grown up religious makes me think."

"You are religious? You are blaming your lostness on religion?"

"Yes to all the above. I just don't know about anything, including about religion. So I am religious without a religion. A hippie without a beard or drugs, sex, and rock and roll and with old-fashioned values. Christianity is part of the confusion in me and where I was brought up it was supposed to be the answer. But still it's part of all this backpacking for me in its own way. The prophets wandered, and in the Bible it says sell all your possessions. But how do you do all this stuff? Even though I sort of am doing some of the wandering and going with few possessions. Yet why should we do it? I even question that, but I love living this way. I don't recommend it, but there's probably something to it. So, the search and the wandering and the living without possessions."

"But Elon, surely by now it is not the same as when you started this questioning. This search. Surely there is advancement in you by now."

"I have learned from both questioning and seeking answers," I agreed.

"What next for you, Elon?"

I looked to the side of her, not knowing how to answer.

"You don't seem spoiled to me, I must say," she said approvingly. "I know it is irresponsible of you to live like this. But you don't seem spoiled, to me. There are so many back home that don't know anything either. I am not sure how much they bother with questions, though. Yes, partying. You used that word 'party.' You are different from them, Elon. I am glad. I worry about Western society. It is nice to find someone who seems to know about the quest, not the party. Of our supposed generation, as you say."

She looked at me more deeply.

"Elon, perhaps it is my farm background, the waking up every day to help milk the cows. As part of the dairy farm we had to feed the animals or help in the fields to raise crops that would feed them. We also had ten hectares of forest. Anyway, things on our farm made us work. Hard. It put my feet on the ground, as they say in America. I also have questions. I also wanted to see other things and to relate to them. Europe, and even America, seem like living in a fantasy to me. We are more like robots than focused. There is still some work ethic remaining. Especially in America. But the rest of the world beyond ours is hungry, Elon. Not just for food, but to pull themselves up. The rest of the world is ready to leave us behind. Someday soon, I fear, we will see them so advanced. We live in a far-off land somehow, in Europe. Somewhere adrift. We don't see this rise coming in the rest of the world. We have lost the desire to overcome struggles. We do try to overcome injustice, but that is the fixation. Injustice is everywhere, somehow, in our minds. Maybe because we only now escaped from feudalism and wars. I don't know, but we are asleep. The world is not asleep. It is another reason I am here. I love seeing this, but it frightens me. I want to go home and sound the alarm. We even have a complex about our former colonies. That could be healthy, but it makes us hate ourselves for injustices we made rather than see the hunger at our doorstep. They are going to leave us behind and not look back. Asia is backward and undeveloped, but it is also the cradle of civilization. It only has to find itself again and develop and we will be left so far behind. It is doing this now. Right before our eyes."

She looked at me more intensely for emphasis.

"Do you not see any of this? Doesn't it make you want to do something? To go home and build and educate? Isn't there an urgency?"

"Yes, I see it," I concurred. "And it does indeed frighten me. But it only gives me more questions. So I need more answers now. That is my urgency. Answers. Questions."

She almost sneered, but then smiled instead.

"You are hopeless, but I think I understand you,

Elon. Yes, you are not like the rest of our generation. You are the epitome of what promise our generation was to have."

She scoped me out further, then leaned intently toward me.

"Tell me, Elon. I don't get it. What possessed someone like you to join the Marines? This hippie that you are should never have joined the Marines. Speaking of not being like the rest of our generation. You are not like anyone. Why? I suddenly have to know. How did you end up in the Marines?"

"I'm old-fashioned. With old-fashioned values and viewpoints. I told you that. I'm not a hippie. Being old-fashioned is what separated me from hippies and our generation. I still believed in the war. The one in Vietnam. It was a controversial war, but they all are. There came out the Pentagon Papers that seemed to disprove the domino theory. The Pentagon Papers said the Communists in Vietnam just wanted their independence against a European colonial power. So therefore, what were we doing there as the latest white supremacist imperial power? But to me that didn't prove anything. They wanted their independence and so it's none of our business? We wanted to give them their independence and tried talking France into giving them that after World War II, when France ruled them. And we wanted England to release their colonies, too. We didn't believe in colonies and were the first to give ours up. We granted the Philippines their independence as soon as World War II was finished. We got talked into taking over the Philippines by all these colonialists in the world. Better us than Germany or Japan, our allies said. Anyway, we didn't believe in imperialism, so we

38

gave our colonies up and pushed Britain and France to give theirs up."

"Then how did you get involved in Vietnam, if that is the case?" she quizzed.

"Because we emerged as the world power. We preferred Western colonial powers to Nazis and Communists, but we still didn't believe in colonialism. Easier said than done. When a Western power moved out, someone else moved in. Russia claimed it just wanted to be free of the czar. But then it decided to liberate its neighbors to its own domination. China just wanted to get rid of Western powers and Japan, so they said. But it ran off Chiang Kai-shek, who was a nationalist, and then saw enemies and imperialists everywhere. It is also mischievous and ambitious. The Korean War started a great deal because of them."

"That's just a power struggle, Elon. What's wrong with that?"

"The result is the problem," I replied. "Not just their economic system, but the millions of massacres, and the tyranny. But it still isn't necessarily our business, though it just may be, some. We at least had sway with our friends. These Communists hate everyone. Even if Russia and China weren't part of a plot to make Vietnam part of some domino theory, the trend was still very frightening in a domino theory way. We decided to make a stand. We even felt obliged, since we were the superpower. We didn't believe in colonialism, Western or Communist. And Communism was brutal beyond measure and spreading. Violently spreading. I believed in that stand against it. To sit passively by and be innocent, while one by one any determined Communist group kept taking over more and more countries? No. It was going to hit home someday."

"So Vietnam was your battle?" she poked.

"It was even more than that," I continued. "Once the war got controversial, you had to do more than follow. You had to think. That's what democracies do anyway. But our generation was so overrated about thinking. Those were very thought-provoking times, for a while, but not for very many people soon after that. Somehow people chose sides instead of thinking. The traditional side or new age. You mostly just had to learn your side and believe you were right. By the time I joined the Marines, not many shared my viewpoint. If some kid came out of high school or college and still was old-fashioned, the rest of our generation straightened him out really quickly. What a dork he was. How his mother talked him into killing Commies and hating minorities and he's too happy with his naïveté. So everybody started getting enlightened. Since I was still old-fashioned, it had to be for no other reason than that I was still naïve. One guy in the Marines with me came in old-fashioned, but soon, right in front of my eyes, became as enlightened as the new age wanted and started taking drugs and being anti-war."

"He heard another side for the first time," Brigitte mused.

"No, not at all. He had heard that side for years, back in his environment, and knew all the arguments against the anti-war crowd while in his fortress called home. But then suddenly he wasn't shielded by home anymore or reinforced by his traditional value insights while they were being constantly attacked by the new age against Marines. New thoughts got forced down his throat. He was challenged full throttle for the first time with no refuge."

"Yes, I know what you mean," she said. "I've seen this also. It doesn't just happen in America or about Vietnam."

"So the point is, Brigitte, challenges are great. But are we up to them or not? In this guy's case, he was not up to the challenge. No side is ever fully right. It is okay to see and agree to something new or at least think about it. But with this guy and so many others, they missed the opportunity from the challenge. It comes out either/or, instead, too easily. There wasn't an original idea in his head, either as a traditional patriot or later as an anti-war enlightened. Meaning he was still the most naïve twerp imaginable. And he decided he was going to enlighten me too, since I was just being stubborn in my naïveté, and since there was nothing to admire or love about America or traditional values, and so on. So why was I holding on to the old, he seemed to think. I just seemed the last All-American boy to him in his tunnel vision."

Brigitte gleamed approval my way and rubbed the bridge of my nose affectionately. She then placed her hand on my cheek to pull it softly toward her to look me in the eye.

"You are your own man for sure, Elon. You are on a search. Then and now."

Chapter 5

I was surprised at how calm I was during my modeling debut. It helped that I didn't take it seriously. I even felt silly being a model. When Brigitte first offered it to me, I was happy to have a job, while modeling itself seemed glamorous, going by what I saw in magazines and television and such. But as soon as I began training for it, it seemed dumb. There are a lot of dumb jobs, but most of them never pass off as glamorous. I wanted to do well and I wanted Brigitte to be glad she hired me, but I quickly felt phony. Even superficial. Modeling had a purpose, but I still felt silly.

The wardrobes I modeled included shirts, slacks, pajamas, and even underwear. I actually had to go out wearing a pressed T-shirt with underwear. I assumed they were expensive, fancy things, but I couldn't tell by looking at them. I walked suavely along a platform, posed on a stage sophisticatedly, and felt like an idiot as I did so. Especially with the flesh-colored ointments to cover any exposed sores. I was so glad when it was over, with Brigitte congratulating me on my performance. That meant I had my second job and I was confident to keep it.

"Let's go celebrate," she said to me as she caressed my upper arm. "Where to, *mon ami*?"

"Same place. But we'll have a wine this time."

This was the latest we had been for our after-hours

meals. There were more people in the folk house we patronized now than during our normal hours there, and we had a hard time finding a table. The singer we had come to enjoy was finished for the evening, with another singer due on stage shortly.

"Look," Brigitte yelped as she focused on a woolly-haired white guy walking onto the stage.

She glanced at me as if amused.

"What's happening in the USA?" the entertainer bellowed out to the microphone as he strapped the guitar around his shoulders. He had a Mid-American accent. "Sit back and enjoy. Joe Cool is here to save your evening."

This introduction caused a chuckle between Brigitte and myself.

"Looking good out there," he continued. "It's party time now. You working-class blokes just applaud when I'm finished singing. All you hip, cool cats rattle your jewelry."

I almost flinched at how corny he was. I looked over at Brigitte.

"Do you recognize what he just said?" I asked her.

"What do you mean, Elon? Just enjoy."

"How can I?" I groaned. "He's not a Joe Cool at all, he's a phony. What's happening in the USA, Joe Cool, and all that stuff. It's trite anymore to hear this talk. Every tired cliché in the books. But the rattle your jewelry crap? Gag."

"Lighten up, Elon. What's wrong? We just had a great night, and now we're here to relax. Chill out, babe. Is 'chill out' trite to you too? I still hear it in American movies. So I still use it. What's wrong with you?"

"Brigitte, don't take up for this idiot. If he wants to be cool, don't be an idiot. This guy is an idiot. Don't you recognize the 'rattle your jewelry' line? That's the Beatles, in particular John Lennon. It was appropriate when he was the first one to say it at a royal invitation concert in London. There's no jewelry here except a few wristbands. And even if they had jewelry, God! That's phony stuff. As if he invented it. You're just using everyday slang when you say 'chill out,' and it's fun. You're not trying to impress me. This guy—"

"Shush, Elon. Please. Just enjoy."

I nodded appeasingly. But if I heard anything like 'Women should be obscene and not heard' from this guy, another John Lennon domain witticism, I was getting up and leaving. After I puked all over the floor.

I had to recognize, however, the way he got applause. He was an entertainer, and it was working. I decided to indeed chill out.

"He's got them going," I moaned in disbelief. "His voice is only so-so."

"Have a good time, Elon."

I grimaced and shook my head, then returned my attention to Joe Cool.

Brigitte applauded after each number, but not as enthusiastically as the crowd. I tried to give him credit for pulling off acceptance by the patrons. *Everyone has an angle, and his is working,* I lectured myself and almost began to enjoy his performance in spite of how phony he still seemed to me.

After another number, Joe Cool scoped out the audience as if looking for someone.

"I notice a couple of Americans in the audience," he said while looking in our direction. "You're overdressed, Dude and Dudette," he said with a chuckle. "You're spoiling it for the working class here, who came to unwind. No stiffs allowed. But stay. Welcome anyway. Joe Cool loves you. And when I asked, you never answered me. So I'll try again. What's happening in the USA, dudes?"

I didn't bother to respond.

"Come on up here, man. Let's have a powwow."

I held up my wine glass, then took a swallow before setting it back down on the table to show I didn't want to bother. I was more entertained by his absurdity than his talent or personality.

"Aw, man, loosen up, amigo," he chirped. "But hang around, I'd like to talk to you after my show. Is that a go?"

I nodded that it was and decided I wanted to find out more about him. Just from curiosity. I wanted to see how he ended up in Taiwan.

"Thanks for hanging around," Joe Cool said to us at our table after his hour on stage was over.

I gave a nod for my reply.

"Are you guys from America?" he asked. "You look American. At least you do, dude." He then looked at Brigitte. "Are you European? You hold yourself differently than Americans. Or Canadians, for that matter. I'm Canadian, and we're a lot like Americans in our style."

"You're Canadian?" I asked him, showing a bit of disdain. I liked Canadians, and there was a lot of overlap in our language and culture, but I had grown to resent how many Canadians held themselves above us in politics and social ideas, then tried to out-American us to be accepted more prominently.

"Yes," he answered. "I'm Canadian and on my way back home, but taking the scenic route. I was at a club in Hong Kong, and they set me up here. I work illegally, to be honest. The club owner back in Hong Kong knew the owner here and persuaded him to let me stay. I'm on my way to Japan to make sex shows. Then I'll go back home."

I managed to hold a straight face, not wanting to give him any satisfaction, thinking he might get off to shocking straights. I hoped he was better in the sex show field than he was as a singer, but maybe the Japanese didn't care.

He turned his attention to Brigitte, who could not hold her grimace.

"That's really what I wanted to talk to you about," he continued. "I need a sex partner for the show."

He then looked at me.

"Are you two an item?" he asked.

All kinds of scenarios rushed through my mind from that question. How should I answer? My first instinct was to protect Brigitte from possible harassment or embarrassment, but I wondered if I should protect myself as well. This guy appeared to have no boundaries or scruples, and smugly so.

"No," I answered. "We're just friends."

"Good," he said matter-of-factly before looking back at Brigitte. "Very good."

I was grateful his interest was in Brigitte and not me.

"They love Americans in Japan. Where did you say you were from again?"

She hesitated, then answered, "Belgium."

"Great," he said with a wide smile. "Europe is even

better. An American—actually Canadian—and a European goddess. You're quite a looker. They'll love you. I've seen videos of some of these shows. Onstage performances in a club or bar. Small intro of us, no time wasted on elaboration. They want to see us get at it. Then we get hot for one another, strip, and start humping. Fondling each other, then you on top, me on top, dog style, oral, sixty-nine. The works. Let me show you."

He got up from his chair to make a demonstration of his role in the scenes. Somehow no one around seemed to notice him except for when he elaborated on the from-behind part.

Was this a joke? My sanity wanted to believe it. I didn't want anyone to be this crazy. This wasn't free or hip—this guy was crazy. But he got his point across. Brigitte knew exactly what she had in store for her if she had any inkling at all to do a sex show in Japan. She looked at me to share the humor, then back at him as she let out a laugh.

"I appreciate your offer, Joe Cool," she said to him. "But I live here and have a job here. Not as good as being a sex queen in Japan, I'm sure, but I'm a model here. That's where we just came from and why we're dressed in business attire. We come here to unwind. It's our first time to see you perform. On stage and off."

"We'll get ten thousand dollars, sweetheart. Ten thousand. That's five each. You don't make that much money here. You can come right back here within the month. This is opportunity, honey. No way you make five thousand modeling in Taiwan in a month. You can't say no, sweetie."

"But it is indeed a no, Joe Cool. You'll find

someone before you leave Taiwan, I am sure. But I head the agency here, and I wouldn't think of leaving them stranded, even tempted as I should be with this great offer. Thanks, Joe Cool, but sorry."

"Modeling agency, you say," he mused. "Would any of your American or European models be interested, you think? Could you tell them, and I'll talk to them if they are interested?"

"They are all Chinese," she replied. She then looked at me with a smirk. "Except for my comrade here. Do the Japanese go for same gender sex shows?"

She held a straight face, then asked me, "Are you interested, Elon? I can spare you for a while if you want to make a quick—or is it a quickie?—five thousand dollars."

I exposed a humored look her way. She was cute indeed.

"I need Western women." Joe Cool emphasized, "European or American, or Australian. I could get Japanese, even Korean or Chinese there. I need American or European, and I need one now so we can leave together from here and know it's a go."

Brigitte shrugged her shoulders apologetically, glanced a quick smirk my way, then forced out a serious look back at Joe Cool.

Any instinct I had to punch this guy out went to the wayside just seeing how cool Brigitte was with him and what an even bigger idiot he looked now.

He scoped us out one last time, then got up to leave. We watched him walk out of the folk house before we were satisfied it was over.

"This is the most I've ever been entertained, I have to admit," I said with a laugh. "I hope I never go through it again, but Taiwan, you are the ultimate. Joe Cool gave me hives, but it was fun. Now that it's over."

Brigitte lifted her wine glass to a toast.

"Cultural interchange, Elon. It keeps us on our toes. You've been uptight the whole night over this guy. Ease up. That was a blast, I must say. Ha. But gag."

I groaned some more, then looked directly at her for dramatic effect.

"Remember me telling you about why I joined the Marines? Then about that guy that was just so sure he saw the light like the rest of our generation and was going to unnaïve me too, if that's a word. Unnaïve, get it? Anyway, Brigitte, I've had about all I can take of the Joe Cools of the world. I came to Taiwan for the true cultural exchange, and now here was Joe Cool to remind me of the *real world* again."

She made ready to say something, then looked the other way.

"When I joined the Marines, Brigitte, all you ever got by then was the Joe Cools of the world. I think that's why I reacted against him so quickly. I have different experiences than you about it, I guess. That twerp naïve guy in the Marines with me wasn't the only idiot I met when I joined. As a matter of fact, right there at the induction center in San Antonio, I faced it. There were only three of us being inducted into the Marines that day. The other two besides me had the choice of Marines or jail. They had some petty crime but had an out if they wanted to join the Marines. That meant I was the only one, in fact, joining the Marines willingly that day, and probably the only one in the whole induction center that wanted to go to Vietnam. As we were waiting while we got processed, some guy with an Arlo Guthrie hat came prancing in. You know, the hat he wore in the movie *Alice's Restaurant*."

"Yes, Elon. I know of it. Everyone knows of that movie."

"Good, so you get the picture. Anyway, he comes in prancing and walks up to the Army staff and almost line for line goes into this Arlo Guthrie rant in the movie, where Arlo Guthrie was trying to get out of the draft by looking psychotic. As I watched this pseudo-Guthrie character, it was just like I thought when I watched the movie—if the Army is so psychotic and baby-killer mode, then why would wanting to kill be a bad thing? Meaning why the show here with this guy? But Arlo Guthrie got out of the draft in the movie by convincing them he was out of his mind. So this guy at the induction center tried the same stunt. If it worked in a cool movie, then what do real Army idiots know, you know? But stupid as servicemen are supposed to be, I guess, somehow the Army staff saw through the ruse and what he was doing. They told him to go sit down. He walked past me, where I was sitting on the outside seat in one of the rows by the aisle, and I stuck out my foot and tripped him. He fell flat on his face and the entire induction center laughed at him. All but me. I looked at him with disgust and waited to see if he wanted to do anything about it. He felt and showed his humiliation. It wasn't so cool after all. Somehow Hollywood lied."

Brigitte burst out in laughter as she shook her head.

"I should have tripped Joe Cool," I said with a sneer. "They're all so phony, Brigitte. Some aren't as phony as Joe Cool, and are easy enough to get along and carry on a conversation with, but they are boring. Boring. Is there an original thought anywhere?"

"It's not that I don't agree with you at all, Elon, and I'm sure you don't mean it as strongly as you ranted just now, but there are things to work out in life. We all have our challenges and frustrations. We must deal with them. You take all this so seriously."

"I'm okay," I replied. "Some of my memories still get to me, though. I guess it's obvious. All the more reason I'm doing what I'm doing now with my travels. Mostly, it's a reaction to going one on one with the Age of Aquarius through the years."

I smiled at her.

"And now I've met you."

Chapter 6

I couldn't get out of bed. My fever persisted and was getting worse. My chest area hurt immensely, enough so that I had trouble breathing.

"We have a complaint about you," the caretaker of the hostel said to me. "The others are afraid. Afraid you are contagious. You must go to the hospital. I will send someone to show you the way. It is not far from here."

I nodded that I understood reality.

"Can you tell Brigitte?" I asked him. "If she doesn't see me in the next day or two she will probably worry about me. Let her know what happened."

I took a change of clothes and my passport, besides what I wore, leaving all else in my locker. I had no idea how long I would be in the hospital.

The walk was painful as I trudged along. The man who showed me the way was patient. He went in with me to help with the staff.

"I don't have much money," I apologized to the receptionist.

I was scared now. Was I going to survive? And how was I going to pay for anything if I did? I wondered if I had a job anymore.

They checked me into a room with three other patients. A doctor I took to be in his thirties looked me over after a nurse washed me down, put me in a patient's robe, and placed me in a single wide bed barely long enough for my Texas body.

"You are in poor condition," the doctor said a few minutes later, telling me what was obvious. "It is these cysts you have. You should have come sooner. Perhaps we could have done something. Now they are lodged on your lungs, I fear, going by your symptoms. We will do an x-ray to be sure, but all the signs are you have a cyst on at least one lung, but I think in both lungs. This is very serious. It could be worse. We are assuming it isn't worse. These bacteria could have lodged in your heart or brain. We will check to make sure they did not. You will be here for several weeks."

As bad as I felt, hearing all this made me feel worse, ready to panic.

My conscience plagued me as I recalled how I had ignored all common sense about my condition. Somehow Mother Nature would take her course, I'd assured myself during my weeks of living in denial. Young and hardy me, a Marine with a good and vibrant immune system. But now that the cold hard facts were upon me, I remembered stories of how more soldiers died in battle from infection than from the gunshot itself. It was sickening to face how stupid I was.

Don't ever do this again, I scolded myself. Assuming I got the chance to do anything again.

I was delirious and fell immediately to sleep after the doctor left. I could hear rustling noises around me. I fought to open my eyes. There was a stand holding a tall iron rod next to my bed. It had plastic tubes hooked up to clear flexible bottles at the top of it.

"You are awake," the doctor said soon after his return. The young nurse with him kept working on the tubes. "Your results are in, and they are bad. The good news is the bacteria did not nest on any other organs, but the bad news is they did attach to both lungs. You are in serious condition. Your temperature is one hundred four. You are near convulsions. Not all that far from death. I am not trying to alarm you, but I must prepare you. We have work to do to get you healthy, and we must start now. These are antibiotics and fluids in the bottles. You are very dehydrated. We also have to enhance your immune system. You are too weak to digest solid food, so we must nourish you intravenously with glucose solutions and vitamins."

"Don't sugarcoat this, Doc," I joked, hoping to not deflate from depression right in front of everyone. "Tell me the blunt truth."

The doctor spent a second registering that I was joking. He then smiled.

"It is good you have humor," he said. "You have spirit. You will need this."

He then waited to see if I had more to say.

"I will be back in an hour to check on you," the doctor assured. "I am leaving you in good hands, with a very caring and knowledgeable nurse—and quite pretty, too, to further raise your spirits."

I nodded and thanked him, then checked out the nurse, who indeed was quite pretty. Asian women easily had an exotic appeal.

Cysts on both lungs. What was I expecting? Even ignorance didn't describe me. Stupid was the perfect word, I decided in disgust.

I heard a noise at the entrance of the room. I eased my head over to look and saw Brigitte approaching my bed, wearing a serious demeanor.

"Hello, my lovely," she said with a smile. She

began to shake her head as the serious look returned to her. "I should have brought you here myself right after the show at the department store instead of celebrating with Joe Cool. I suppose even then it was too late. They say you have cysts on both of your lungs. I am sure they had already placed by the fashion show we did, but perhaps not so harshly then. Maybe we could have avoided the full brunt if I would have just made you come here immediately. But you would not have come, my dear. You think you are somehow indestructible."

She felt my forehead with her hand.

"Oh, Elon," she moaned. "My dear. Oh, my dear. I could cook an egg right here with your body as my stovetop. I cannot believe I let you do this to yourself. Somehow, even as concerned as I was about you, I gave you too much benefit of the doubt. You were in terrible shape right in front of me, just able to function, and somehow I thought this manly man could conquer the odds. But you indeed are not indestructible, Monsieur Texan. Never again will I allow you to think this about yourself. I won't baby you but instead will bully you when I must."

She began to stroke my cheek with affection.

"I don't want to depress you further, my dear, but I must be blunt. With a purpose. Your hospital bill will be several thousand US dollars, however much in New Taiwan dollars is the equivalent. I paid the first one thousand. So do not worry. You do not owe me. But I needed to assure the hospital you would pay the bill. They are very conscientious. They will treat you. But I wanted to make sure they fully treated you and not fear losing thousands of dollars because of you. Trust me. I had to do this. I know this concerns you, but let it also be a relief to you. We will find a way to pay the bill."

As depressing as the news was, I was comforted by seeing how Brigitte cared so much for me. I was taken care of, and that perked me up. But how was I going to get this kind of money? Especially here in Taiwan as a part-time lackey.

Brigitte pulled off her backpack and brought out a pocket-sized transistor radio.

"Here," she said, laying it next to me. "Listen to music during your long boring hours of recovery. I have an earplug for you so you won't disturb the rest of the hospital. And I already have your favorite song picked out for you. One written as if just for you. Time and fate, my dear fellow. There is a singer from America, Gloria Gaynor. I never heard of her before. But she has a hot new single out now. 'I Will Survive' it is called. As if written for you. You will be inspired to survive now. No excuses."

Affection oozed from her. She seemed pure earth mother as she smiled down and stroked my hair. She cared about me. I managed a pained smile toward her.

"While we are talking about awkward things, mon cheri," Brigitte continued. "At a bad moment, but absolutely the perfect moment. Earlier, I checked on you, but you were asleep. The nurse explained to me about your condition and how long for your recovery. I went to the hostel where you stay. I told them I would come back to gather your things. I will need your lock combination to get your possessions. I want you to move in with me upon your release from the hospital. It will save you money, and I can check on you also. Don't tell me that you don't need this concern from me. Let it attack your pride if it does, but I am with you now. Is that understood? You are indeed independent and almost indestructible. But lying before me in bed now is the rest of the story. It will not be business as usual from now on, and I will enforce this new policy even if you object, which you dare not."

She again rubbed my hair affectionately.

"I care for you, Elon," she went on just above a whisper. "I care greatly for you. So please, let me be your companion. We both fear attachment at this setting of our lives. But life has a say about us also, not just our own simple follies about things. Life has given us a nudge in another direction now. One we did not foresee or plan. Your crisis now is working somehow as a crossroads about us. About you and me."

She looked at me with some confusion.

"Crossroads is not the word," she mumbled. "What is the word about how something changes things? Speeds up change because something happens. Or an ingredient makes a change."

"Catalyst," I replied.

"Yes, that is the word. Catalyst. Beyond our simple relationship and the affection that evolved from it, a catalyst has occurred. For I'm afraid, my dear, I am already fond of you. Indeed, I am very attached to you now. So with these circumstances, we need each other. I need to take care of you and you need to be taken care of, at least in some ways. Quite a shock to you, I know. I am not being bold. Please honor my wishes."

I stared at her for a moment, then turned away and closed my eyes. There was still this independent side of me, but it was small compared with how I wanted her. Maybe it was my vulnerable situation mixed with what feelings I already had for her, but it was all there confronting me now. I felt grateful she asked me into her life.

I stayed on the glucose solution for three days. I did not eat a meal during that time. Strictly glucose directed into my veins. It felt strange to never be hungry.

Within days I felt better. The antibiotics were working. The pain diminished and energy returned.

Brigitte was not the only one visiting me daily.

"How are you?" Mr. Chu asked me. "My wife prepared a meal for you, now that you are able to eat solid food again. You had quite a bad experience. I know about hospital food. There is never enough and it is not very enjoyable."

"Thank you, Mr. Chu," I said. His kindness touched me.

"The hospital told me you will be here for a while. I will visit you every day to see how you are. I want to assure you I still need you when you are fit and about. I will bring you a meal with me. You will be well in no time."

Mr. Chu's visits weren't just reassuring, since I was desperately broke, but I appreciated his follow-through and thoughtfulness. Also, his food was indeed better than the hospital food. I looked forward to his meals each day. Soon I felt as if I was starving without them if he was late in their bringing.

The better I got, the more I longed for Brigitte. Her radio helped, especially when I heard the song she themed for me being played. It was a raging hit. I couldn't get it out of my head each day after I heard it again. But even the radio failed to distract the longing I felt waiting every day to see her. I was falling in love. It wasn't just my vulnerability and weakness, nor her caring. It was everything about her. Her warmth, looks, personality, and her ability to carry on a good conversation about anything. Even her seductive French accent. Our situation egged things on all the more. This remote, developing, semi-tropical island in the Pacific where we shared our lives together—how it fought to turn its economic fortunes around, and survive threats from mainland China also. Somehow our survivals were excitingly all intertwined. Lovingly.

Chapter 7

Brigitte's flat was small, even for a studio, containing a dining and kitchenette area attached to the side of a living room space, which blended in with her bedroom space. She had barely the most simple and practical furniture. The only additional enclosure was a restroom with shower. She didn't need much more, I decided, but since everything was so cheap in Taiwan, I had pictured something bigger for her. It was to the point, in fact. Even a statement of sorts. Accommodation for herself as if just passing through. Don't get too attached. A bit of comfort, nothing more.

"Welcome," Brigitte greeted me as we walked through her door together. "It's not much, but a step up from your circumstances, I suppose."

Her smile especially charmed me. It seemed happy to have me here with her in her domain.

"Would you like to walk around outside?" she beckoned. "To get a feel for your new environment? It's not far from the hostel where you were before. I'm not sure what you've seen already of this area or of Taipei, but I would love to show you around. I really love it here. This part of Taipei, for sure. It's not far from the Imperial Palace. We wouldn't want to walk there. We could walk, but we would sweat to death, and I'm sure you are not in shape to walk much on your first day out of the hospital. Have you seen the palace yet? It's really a museum, I should say."

"I rode a bus by it," I replied. "I didn't get off the bus, but I knew I would want to see it someday. But you are right. I'm already fatigued from just the little bit of walking to your car and up your stairs to your apartment. I am in horrible shape now."

"Maybe you would like to have dinner here tonight," she offered. "And rest then. Just the two of us. This is your apartment, Elon, for as long as you like. We will live day to day. Welcome home. Are you comfortable with this?"

She seemed vulnerable as she asked. It melted me to see this in her.

"I'm happy to be here, Brigitte. I don't know why you've done all this for me, but I am happy you did. And I owe you so much money. I may have to go home and get a job eventually to pay it all off."

She flinched. I assumed, even hoped, that was because I mentioned going home someday.

"We will live cheaply, Elon. You still are teaching English and you still are with me in modeling. You have free rent and the food is very inexpensive here. You will be fine. Be patient for now with how things are. I am patient about this. Let's not talk about going home. That will happen on its own someday soon enough."

"Will I be able to keep working, though, Brigitte? I haven't been to Mandarin class for the three weeks I was in the hospital. I couldn't possibly go back and try to catch up. I don't know when another class will begin."

"But you still have your student visa. That is good for several months. You are fine for now. So let's live day to day, just as we spoke."

"I was using their weight room for workouts, too,"
I added. "And their track for jogging. I need to get back
into shape quickly. I am so weak now."

"But you still have your muscles," she said as she
inspected me. "Yes, they have shriveled a bit, but only
some. You will be in shape quickly. Be patient. That
word again. Be patient. We have nothing but time. You
can still use the university facilities. On paper you are
still a student. Let's just start our life now. We will
solve any problems. Is that a plan, mon cheri?
Challenge. Our life is full of challenge. Challenge is
fun."

All this boldness came out so calmly from her, so
naturally.

"You go relax now, my dear," she said
reassuringly. "Lie down on the bed or sit on the couch.
Let me cook us something if we are going to stay here
for the rest of the day."

She casually looked at the bed, then at me.

"Elon, I am taking some things for granted about
us. I am not being pushy or forward. Or perhaps I am,
but please. I have but one bed. It is rather narrow. One
and a half width. I have no mattress for you separate,
and the couch is too small for you to stretch out. I hope
you are comfortable with this prospect of sleeping with
me. I know everything is sudden. But life forced our
hand, as the saying goes. I have been the one preparing
for you, thinking about things. You had to recover and
consider consequences of your illness and the
interruption in your life. I am not being aggressive now,
in other words. I hope we can talk about this. But there
has been an attraction from each of us since the very

beginning that was taking a natural growth. Then you got so sick and that changed everything. We are now where we are. And we are adults, yes? In a modern setting of our times. Yes, that is our bed. We will not push things about such, nor will we have to. Mother Nature has a mind of her own. We know what will happen and happen soon and naturally so."

She searched for more to say, but hesitated.

All this indeed was sudden to me, but I was catching up quickly.

As I returned to work, however, a cloud appeared to complicate things.

"Elon," Mr. Chu said to me. "Do you remember the girl, the daughter of the industrialist, the one you taught once and then asked not to teach again?"

I studied him. This wasn't going to be good somehow.

"Yuanjing," I said.

"Yes, that is her. She wants only you to be her teacher. She was not happy when I told her about getting a new teacher. I even used your hospital stay as an excuse, hoping not to lose her as a client. But she wants only you to teach her and she waited the entire three weeks you were in the hospital, just for you. When she heard you had returned to our school, she asked for you again. She even doubled her payments. I can give you more also, if you will only take her. Please, Elon, I ask this as a favor."

Mr. Chu had been so good to me, I could not tell him no. Even if he hadn't done so much I would have done him the favor.

"Sure," I answered. "That's fine. I'll be happy to have her, and you don't have to pay me extra."

"That is wonderful, Elon. I will tell her. I will also pay you extra."

He shook my hand in appreciation.

How was I going to handle this?

Chapter 8

"Here is a letter for you," Brigitte said handing it to me.

I took it and immediately looked at the return address.

"It's from Texas," I said, amazed. "My mother. I've been out of contact for half a year or so. She didn't know I was in Taiwan, much less at this address."

"I wrote her," Brigitte explained. "Soon after you entered the hospital. Soon after I moved your things to my apartment. I did not tell her of such an arrangement. That was not the purpose. But as I went through your belongings and the letters, I decided I must write anyone that may have concerns about you. I saw a letter from Texas from your family. I did not read it. I am not nosy, but I felt I should explain your predicament. I mentioned nothing about the hospital bill. I just wanted to let her know of your condition. You were improving when I wrote my letter, already off of IV glucose solutions and eating solid food. Reason for optimism. Is that all right with you, Elon? Perhaps I should have told you, but this is why you have this letter now. I am sure it is answering my explanation of your condition."

I nodded approval of her explanation, then opened the letter. It was several pages long, so I sat on the couch to read it. Brigitte brought me a cup of coffee as I did so.

"My parents lost the farm," I said in a distant way, still trying to get my bearings from all the news back home. "We were middle class. We farmed several hundred acres, but this is Texas. Everyone farmed a lot of acres. It was good soil, too, with water for irrigation. Sort of like if you can't make it there, you can't make it. And suddenly, after generations, we didn't make it."

Brigitte showed her concern as she sat next to me.

"I don't know what it takes to make it," I sighed in a depressed tone while shaking my head. "America is the most productive and efficient agricultural country in the world. That's what I read anyway, and even studied about it in college."

I looked at her to share my discomfort.

"I guess it's just as well I didn't stay home and take over the farm. But it was still an option, and I considered doing that someday."

"So what will they do?" Brigitte asked.

"We owned about a hundred acres. We can sell that or rent it out. And sell the farm equipment. My mother is a schoolteacher, so that's a salary at least. My dad now works as a foreman on a feedlot. So that's more money."

"What is a feedlot?" Brigitte asked.

"That's to fatten cattle. When a rancher is ready to market his cattle, the last stage is to fatten them up a few weeks at a feedlot. You cram all these cattle into a pen. They can't walk around much, just eat fatty grains and lie around getting fat. Then you slaughter them. So he has some sort of job, at least. They'll survive. I suppose even stay middle class. Still, it's depressing."

"If agriculture is productive and efficient," Brigitte asked, "how did this happen?"

"Everyone struggles," I explained. "We never had any extra money, even with all the government subsidies."

I looked at her to see if she understood what I was talking about.

"We got paid for not growing too much cotton," I explained further.

"They paid you to not grow cotton?" Brigitte asked incredulously.

"To stabilize the market," I informed.

"We also get paid subsidies on our farm in Belgium," she said. "We have good land in Europe also, and usually water, but we get subsidies because of security. Europe has had so many wars. We have small countries in Europe, compared to America, China, and Russia, anyway. And if there is a war or a trade boycott, we want to make sure we have local food production. So our governments pay our thousands of small farmers to produce. My family would also go bankrupt, like many of us, without these subsidies."

"I don't really believe in subsidies," I said. "I know it doesn't make sense since my family got them for decades and they helped us survive."

"Why would you not believe in subsidies?" she quizzed.

"Subsidies came as part of the New Deal before World War II," I answered as I pieced my thoughts together. "There was a depression and no place for our millions of farmers to go if they lost their farms. So the government tried to control production and prices and stabilize the labor market at the same time. They used subsidies, price guarantees, and production limits as part of the strategy, to manipulate the marketplace. It was all based on supply and demand. We're way past that now, and we produce so much we don't really have to worry about trade wars or war overseas. We're the world's biggest exporter of agricultural goods."

I looked up at her to show my frustration.

"I love the family farm and was always grateful for subsidies. I just know there is no real reason to have them and it depends on other people's tax money. But I was glad for our farm and the whole community. Farm communities. Farm culture and society. But farmers are leaving or losing their farms anyway. Now us. I can't go home and farm now. There are so many struggling back home. It wasn't just us struggling that was the problem. What happened to my dad, though, was he sold all his grain to a local rancher. That's how my mother explained it just now. A successful one, so he thought. The guy gave him a decent price and bought in bulk. Except after my dad delivered the grain, the rancher didn't pay. He made a down payment, then defaulted on the rest. My dad punched him out over it after a year of not getting paid. We had already lost the farm by then."

"I am sorry to hear this sad story, Elon. But at least your parents have jobs and you are here. It is one less option for you, but you will find your way. It is best to know the situation now."

"The world is scary," I said with a heavy tone. "We're the richest and most productive country, but things happen anyway. Even with the government trying to keep it from happening."

"Yes," Brigitte reinforced, "the world is very scary. As we often talked in our conversations before you went to the hospital almost penniless. So it is not calmer now, with your problems."

I replied, "That sense of urgency you were talking about? It feels so much more urgent now. I wanted answers. Well, I'm getting some. Some I already knew. Or thought I knew. But that's why I'm here, like I said. I need so much more depth even for the answers I had."

I thought for a few moments, silent.

"Urgency," I repeated. "Urgency. This puts more focus on things. I'm glad."

"Does it change things for you, Elon?"

I nodded that it did.

"But I don't know what yet," I said. "More to work on."

"Did your mother not talk about your health?"

"Sure," I answered. "She started off with that. I know I'm healthy now, though, and then she hit me with the bad news about the farm. So that got my attention."

"What did she say? Is she worried about you? You should immediately let her know you are okay. And again employed. Don't talk about your debt. That is our concern. Don't worry her. Just assure her you are all right."

"I'm even more indebted to you now," I said. "They're in no shape to help me. They not only lost the farm, but it was over money. They are making it, we always do, but I can't bother them with my problems."

I sighed and looked at her for empathy.

"All that urgency we talked about…" I said with a moan. "I'm haunted by it now. Yes, all this scares me. What are we going to do, Brigitte? We're seeing all these Asian economic tigers on the rise. We're living in one of them now."

"They are small countries," Brigitte said. "Small enough that even if we bother to notice them, we still feel so secure and smug. No need for concern, we seem to think. Even Japan is not that big, though bigger than the rest of the tigers. But Japan had a vast and mighty empire before they lost it during the war. Now look. It is on the rise again. Now China. With Mao gone, they are not the same mindset as before."

"Deng Xiaoping, you mean," I concurred. "He's apparently not the new chairman of the Communist Party, but somehow he's the new Communist head of state in some kind of de facto sense. I'm not sure what's going on there, but he's the one you hear mostly about. Economically, Deng is a free market guy. He even had Mao's widow arrested when she complained. And China is not at all small. They are one of the countries we were talking about, with a history of civilization. So Deng has much of Mao's former power, but he gets the picture of what it takes economically. With China's history and vastness, and with that urgency and hunger we talked about, yes, China is just beginning to be a tiger."

I made a fake shiver.

"Urgency, Brigitte. I feel all this urgency."

"So what now, Elon? What is going on in that head of yours with this new development in your life?"

"Answers, Brigitte. Answers. An even bigger urgency for answers."

I stared at her as my affection grew toward her.

"I need you, Brigitte. Exactly you. I'm more focused now. Because of you."

"That's how it works, Elon. Here is yet another catalyst thrown our way. It's good to make plans, but life has the biggest say. It often overrules us."

"So what will we do, Brigitte? And I don't mean about life. I mean about us. You and me. Here we are. I want more of us. I want where we're headed. Wherever that is."

Chapter 9

"Come to training," Brigitte encouraged me. "You were able to run a half mile yesterday. You have enough endurance for training. Trainings are easy. You've seen this. It will help remind you what to do with a fashion show, also. It is time. You've been teaching English for a week now. This will help get you back into saving money. Especially with no rent to pay. You will be out of debt to me soon."

"I'll never pay off my debt to you," I whined.

"Never mind, then, if that happens. But yes, you will."

"I need another job," I said. "Since I don't live in the hostel anymore, is there going to be any movie scout find me? How am I going to be discovered?"

"I know some people. What do you think? I am a model running an agency. They always come to me. First, do another show. Let's see how you are, if you are ready."

I felt the frustration from my physical setback and the lost muscle definition. A year before, I was able to run three miles a day, even six or more at times. I could bench press three hundred pounds, more than one and a half times my body weight. But I weighed only a hundred seventy-five pounds when I checked out of the hospital and had now managed to put only a couple of pounds back. I was beyond slim for my six-foot-three frame.

With my schedule, I had several hours to myself during the day. Most of my classes were at night, to compensate for the work hours and school needs of so many of my students. Brigitte's schedule was haphazard. She had a few hours fixed, but usually met with clients at any time.

If I wasn't working out or reading, I often watched television. There were many Kung Fu melodramas that I couldn't stand. There were occasional Chinese operas, which greatly fascinated me with their songs, style, and costumes. But mostly I watched American shows, and there were many of them, lucky for me. I loved watching *Loveboat* when Brigitte was with me, but didn't care for it much alone. I always watched *The Donny and Marie Osmond Show*, corny as they were.

Constantly, the feel of urgency found its way to me as I watched the TV shows, the urgency that often haunted both myself and Brigitte. All the American shows contained both Chinese and English subtitles. Big bold English words for the locals to read even while the show spoke those English words. The main purpose of the shows, even over the entertainment factor, was for studying English, in fact. To help engrain English in someone enough for them to go to an American university, or to find a job in the U.S., or even to compete better in the world market using the international medium, which was English.

I wanted Brigitte with me as I felt the angst inside as I watched.

So if I felt so much urgency, why wasn't I ready to go home, I wondered. I knew the answer to that— because there was more to see and experience.

Concerns were rampant inside me about the world I lived in. This was a makeshift, hands-on laboratory for me to experience and learn from, and living it gave me confidence along the way. It was street-wise school.

"I talked to a movie agent," Brigitte informed me later that night when I returned from teaching. "There is a movie now with a setting in America. San Francisco's Chinatown. A Taiwan immigrant's story in America. This guy is in trouble with the law and has to show up in court. So they need an American for the judge part in the movie. You are a bit young for that role, but the agent will overlook it. They will dress you in a robe and put a mustache on you or something to help age you. Anyway, you must sit there looking distinguished and judicial. You listen to all the arguments. A Taiwanese will play the part of the lawyer for the immigrant. You take everything in, then somewhere you have a line. Something like, "*It is the judgment of the court to put you away forever*," or whatever it is you will say. That simple. But, Elon, it is your first part. Don't overact. I know you will not do a big dramatic Shakespeare bravado, but do not overact at all. Just be normal. Cool. Like now."

"The simple part for me in the movie is great," I said appreciatively. "But it means not much money."

"That's what we have for now, Elon."

I nodded my head knowingly.

"It's still a few minutes of a scene, and a speaking part, too," she assured me, "however minimal. That makes you a bit actor and not an extra. So be grateful for that. You will make more money than as an extra."

I thought for a moment while digesting it all.

"Yeah, okay, I know. Thanks. I'm grateful for it.

Just grabbing all I can for now."

"It all helps," she encouraged. "But to me it is exciting, Elon. I love the adventure of surviving. You were a lone wolf survivor before I met you. I am here now with you. We both are still surviving. This is what surviving is. However you get a break. Whatever it takes. You would survive without me here, but I am helping, and it makes us partners. I love this. I never had a partner before. I have colleagues, where we have a network of sorts. But you and I are partners. I love it."

She looked at me starry-eyed, then leaned toward me to kiss in celebration.

"Partners, Elon. Partners."

I hugged her as a reply, then pulled back to look at her in a serious way.

"How did you get here, Brigitte? You didn't just bop here from your farm and start modeling."

"Yes, I did," she replied with a grin. "Not quite, I admit. You are correct somewhat in your assessment. I was a university student. Just as I finished my university degree, I met a girl who had done this. She wasn't head of an agency, though. At first, she worked for a British firm in Hong Kong, then visited Taiwan and was asked if she could model during her visit by the former head of the agency I now work for. The agency head was very much like me, meaning always on the look for an attractive white person. My friend was tall, slim and attractive. My friend later told me of her time doing this and threw it out to me in an adventurous way. How I could start as a model and learn Mandarin in a university to get my work visa. My company here later got me a residency work visa. In America you would say a green card. All this appealed

75

to me. I came here on a whim, for adventure, just from this conversation with this girl in Belgium about her days as a model here. What did I have to lose? If it didn't work out, I could go back home. I can teach English in the meantime, on the economy, and experience while learning some Mandarin. Mandarin can be helpful in the business world. There are Chinese businessmen all over Asia. Such an exciting thought for me just out of university."

"You came, you saw, and you conquered," I said on her behalf.

"I came to a world I never lived before," she said from the memory. "Everything until then had been growing up on a dairy farm and being a university student. When I arrived here, I felt the spirit. The wanting-to-make-it spirit. I stayed and worked my way up. I was lucky, too. Luck is part of surviving. After a few months, the girl that ran the agency—she was the most beautiful Chinese girl in Taipei—found work in Canada with a Hong Kong-owned company. We were good friends and she was impressed with me. Also I had university education. And so…"

Brigitte shrugged as if to finish the sentence.

"And now," she said as she put her arms tightly around my neck, "phase three, you might say. From novice model to agency head, and now partners with Elon. What next for us? I am glad I do not know. It would spoil things to know."

"Yeah, well, I'm glad you think we're partners," I said with a grimace. "But it's more like you're my manager. I agree with the survivor angle. You do what you do to survive, so I don't mind you coming to my rescue on this phase of the game for me, but that doesn't make us partners. It makes you my rescuer while I'm the survivor."

"Manager is a better word for me," she said with a tease. "Stick with that word. I'm your manager. But hear me out, mon cheri. We are partners. I have broadened my horizons by lending you money, interest free, my goodness. What kind of financier is this? And I have taken you in and helped you find work. Then made incredible love every night with you. A bonus. I hope a bonus for you also. But partners in this lovemaking feast. You could have done all of this without me. Except for the lovemaking, of course. You already met the people that run the hostel here where you stayed. They already told you about teaching English and introduced you to the owner of the English school where you work. And about getting a student visa to do all of this. You could have done all of this without me. Eventually even the movie making."

"I wouldn't be modeling, and I couldn't have paid the hospital," I interrupted her.

"So all this is for you to pay me back. Our partnership. You are doing this paying back. So you are a client—"

"Dependent," I corrected.

"You are a client," she repeated. "Also, in my latest business venture, a partner. I find you work, you pay me back. That is a partnership, no?"

I grinned at the analysis. May as well go along.

"Our partnership will make more sense to you someday, Elon. You give me romantic fulfillment as part of the deal."

"Don't make me feel like a prostitute," I said with a bite.

"No, no, Elon. I said fulfillment. I meant fulfillment. I am happy. I live such a happy life now. I did before, but now fulfilled. You share my life. My heart."

With that she chewed on her lower lip and exposed vulnerability.

I wanted to say corny things to her, but stroked her cheek with affection instead.

Chapter 10

I saw the puzzled expression on one of my students as she stopped reading aloud to look at me. This girl asked a lot of questions. I liked her curious mind, but I was always nervous about having a good answer.

"Why does the e not pronounce at the end of so many words? For instance, when I read the word 'quite,' I am not supposed to pronounce the e at the end of it. Then why do they put it there?"

"What happens when you take off the e at the end?" I replied, knowing I had an answer of some sort for her.

She thought for a moment.

"Go ahead," I coaxed her. "Spell it. Spell it without the e at the end."

"Q-U-I-T," she pronounced.

"What does that spell?"

"Quit. Like I quit going to the bank because I have no money."

The small class laughed at her example, as did she.

"So," I explained, "without the e we have a totally different word. Not just the same word pronounced differently, but a totally different word with a different meaning."

The girl looked at me unconvinced.

"They could still pronounce quite as quitee," she said in a lecturing manner.

"Too much hassle," I replied. "So you're suggesting quite pronounced as quit and then pronounce the e at the end as a long e or something. That's an extra syllable and sounds too much like quit too. So whoever decided this through the millennia came up with some system that defaults to this—if there is a word that ends in e, then the vowel inside the preceding syllable is pronounced with a long sound. Otherwise that same vowel has a short sound. And they are completely different words. So, in this case, the e at the end is like a mystically coded message, that the preceding syllable has a long vowel."

I looked at them pointedly to follow through on my explanation, as if to say, surely that makes sense to you now. I needed all kinds of help to get through my classes and the sometimes complicated discussions.

"Then why," she continued further, "is 'lose' not pronounced lows?"

I wanted to hug her for her astuteness, and stick out my tongue at her for the trouble she caused me. I had to think about it, but if I thought very long I would look as dumb as I felt.

'There is also the word 'loose,'" I replied, stalling as much as possible while I thought about this, and wanting to look like I knew something on the subject too. "Two o's together sounds like ew, but in a short spurt sound. 'Lose,' with one o, sounds like ew but a long drawn-out sound."

She nodded as if following my explanation, but she wasn't letting go of this.

"Then why is 'lose' not pronounced 'lows,'" she repeated.

"English can be confusing," I answered. "'Lose' is

an exception to the rule and there is always some exception to the rule somewhere in English. All I can tell you is a silent e at the end of a sentence means the vowel in the syllable preceding it is long. That's the best I can do. So remember the exceptions with practice and experience."

She stared blankly at me, as did the class.

"And there is a p and h and they sound like f," the guy next to her said with a whine. "P doesn't sound like f and h doesn't sound like f even if you put them together. But here they are together and we have to memorize that it means f sound. If English already has an f that sounds like f, then why also p and h to sound the same way? I do not understand this. English is as bad as Mandarin, but in a different way bad. I hoped the British were smarter. They conquered the world. Now the Americans dominate the world with their English. But the language is crazy no matter who speaks it."

"What is the English derogatory word for the Chinese people?" another student asked me as if from a different world. This man was a colonel in the Taiwanese Air Force. He was a very cool, calm, and collected man, but not in a stiff way. He seemed intelligent and I liked him.

I thought for a moment about what he said. I knew the derogatory word, but this could get me in trouble. Class had run so smoothly to this point. The readings were seldom interrupted until now. Suddenly, the floodgates of inquiry were let loose.

"Every language and culture has these words," the colonel continued. "Do not be timid to say. It is not about you being a racist. Every culture has derogatory words."

"Chink," I answered him.

He nodded while he mused.

"As in Chin dynasty, or Ching dynasty, or China," he surmised. "This makes sense to me and is not so slanderous either. A foreign people come to your borders, or are in the news, and a culture grabs the few words it knows and slanders in some form. Chink makes sense. What about the Japanese?"

"Nip," I replied.

"From Nippon, their ancient local self-description. It is still used. That is not bad at all. Not like you seem to do to your own people. I suppose it is more personal with one's own people. But also it depends on how badly you use the word. You can be disrespectful with your intention no matter what words one uses."

He seemed satisfied with his own ideas and let the subject subside. I was glad I'd survived another class.

That was a good way to end the session. Time was up, and I let them chew on our discussions as they went home.

It was midmorning now. I had one more session, and my day was complete. That left time for a good workout and run. That was the good news. The bad news was this session was with the daughter of the industrialist, Yuanjing, or Jean. As far as I was concerned, my time with her was a waste, except for the business part of it. Money. I managed to get her to read some, but mostly she still wanted to talk. As much as possible, I diverted attention away from me being American and her wanting to go there, but every class with her was spent a lot on that anyway. I wondered what all she had in store for our version of a semester, but I was pretty sure I knew the wrappings of it. She obviously wanted to go to America with me someday, I was sure soon, and common sense said somehow that meant she wanted to marry me. If so, were we to be married here, or there? To get her into America it probably meant getting married here, in her mind. That made me all the more determined to not encourage her thinking.

"It is lunch time now," Jean said to me. "Our session is over. I was going to eat at a very good restaurant. Do you have a favorite? This one is very nice. A very expensive restaurant with a nice atmosphere. Would you like to go with me? I will pay. I very much enjoy the steak there. Shall we?"

I had not been to a nice restaurant yet. Steak also had an appeal. Plus, it would make this lucrative client happy, and thus my boss. Was this being unfaithful to Brigitte?

"Okay," I said to Jean with a smile.

Part of me now liked this girl. She was sweet. I still thought of her as a brat because she annoyed me with her advances, subtle though they were. She was so confident of herself. Like locking me in with her plans was a given. Still, she had a pleasant personality that mellowed me to her the more I got to know her.

She took me to a part of Taipei I had never been to as yet. I thought Taipei pretty, except for the smog, and was glad to see more of it.

When we arrived, Jean led me to a table in the center of the restaurant. She seemed at ease with herself. She placed both of our orders in Mandarin with the waiter and let me know it was what we would call a T-bone steak back home.

"I am glad you came with me," she said. "I wanted

83

to bring you here for a time. Since we first met. I am glad we are finally here together."

There were windows all around the walls of the restaurant. Luxury hotels could be seen, as well as plush apartment buildings. I felt special being here, like I was sure she hoped.

A salad was brought out as we waited, along with a glass of red wine.

"Did you enjoy?" she asked me after we finished.

"Yes, I did," I answered enthusiastically. "It was a treat for me. I haven't been in a nice place since I left Europe almost a year ago. Thank you very much."

"That makes me happy," she said with a smile.

As we got up to leave, I glanced at her plate. She really was going to leave all that food on her plate. Only half of her steak had been eaten and it meant nothing to her. I was a farm boy. A Texas farm boy, in fact. That steer had been killed for our betterment and enjoyment, but here was this half of a steak cast aside, as if it meant nothing. I thought of our poor cattle back home and wanted to apologize to them.

This made Jean seem all the more a spoiled rich kid.

Chapter 11

I saw the leeriness increase on Brigitte's face the more I told her about my lunch with Jean. Was honesty really the best policy? She soon held up her hand, palm toward me, as if to tell me to stop talking.

"It was a business lunch," she said, forcing out the words while turning to look to the side of me. "I have them all the time. I considered telling you, but you already know I have contacts and means of dealing with people."

She looked back at me.

"So I should understand," she said with a sneer. Her gaze eased toward the floor as if in contemplation, then back at me. "I do understand." She let out a chuckle. "I think. Some of my business contacts are good-looking, some charming. But it's all business. They aren't trying to seduce me." Her stare intensified. "So I am to understand this with you and this woman and have nothing to worry about. Is that right? My clients don't try to seduce me and yours do. But I'm supposed to understand."

She grabbed me by the earlobes.

"I didn't know I was this possessive," she said with another chuckle. "You have an independence about you. I already knew that. It's the first thing that attracted me to you, in fact. Right there at the airport, when I first saw you. But now I worry about just how independent you are."

"I'm independent," I said mockingly. "Right. I live with you rent free, owe you thousands, but somehow I'm independent. I'm glad I told you all this about the girl, though. You have nothing to worry about. I wouldn't want her anyway. She's too young and inexperienced, except for getting what she wants up to now. I don't know what to do with my life. I could never make her happy under my circumstances. She just has this vision of being with an American where everybody is rich and full of promise. I don't know what all she thinks, really, but some of that, I'm sure. Anyway, I'm not interested in her. I never would have been, and now most assuredly I am not, because of you. I don't know what to do about you and me either, except experience life together and see where we're headed. Whether we're going somewhere or not."

She let go of my earlobes to leer at me more.

"Where we're headed," she repeated my words. "Yes. Wherever that is."

"I'll probably need more business lunches with her," I added. "But that's as far as it goes. My boss needs customers like her. I really do want to help him. But I'm not interested in this girl, and I want you and will be loyal to you. I will not encourage her besides accepting lunch now and then. Then she'll see me gone without her."

Brigitte shook her head.

"I'm really possessive," she said again about herself. "My God, how did I not know? I guess you're such a part of me now. Like some vital organ. I don't know. I'm not making excuses, just trying to understand it."

She shook her head in small jerks.

"I promise you too, Elon. I will never cheat on you. I mean it. This matters. I'm glad this happened too. I'm learning more about myself. And us."

The confrontation with Brigitte over Jean sealed something inside. It gave me confidence about us. Suddenly, I felt happy to be tied down. Someone I cared for and respected gave meaning and fulfillment to my life that I hadn't realized I wanted—until now. She said as much by feeling possessive about me. I had always assumed being possessive was a bad thing. Like being selfish and narrow, even weak. Instead, I felt wanted and needed by her, and I loved it. She had feelings for me. No doubt about it. Strong ones. I remembered my feelings for her in the hospital. I sensed more pronounced feelings inside of me now for her. We were able to hurt each other. How wonderful.

As if to celebrate, we went out to enjoy ourselves. But this time we went to a different folk house, as we wanted nothing to do with Joe Cool again.

No one was on stage as we walked in. There was equipment, however, and the place was crowded.

"Look, Elon," Brigitte finally said, pointing to a sign at the back of the stage as we settled ourselves. "They are going to have a karaoke contest tonight. It's even written in English. As if they hope for all comers."

"Do they offer prizes?" I asked.

"Why?" she mused. "Are you interested?"

"Maybe," I answered.

"You're serious."

"I need money," I told her bluntly. "Seems like you'd know that since you need me to pay you back."

A young man came out to announce the contest. He

did so in English.

"Excuse me," Brigitte said to a woman at the table behind us. "This contest tonight. Do they do it often? Are there prizes?"

The girl looked up at Brigitte.

"No prizes," she replied. "The owner sometimes has contests for entertainment, but also to see if there is new talent he might be interested in."

Brigitte looked at me, thoughts seemingly churned inside her head.

"What makes you think you can sing?" she asked me.

"Because I can."

She kept her stare my way, waiting for more explanation.

"I've sung before. Never for a living. Yet. But I got good responses in the past when I sang. Now's the time to start singing for a living."

A sparkle appeared in Brigitte's eyes.

"You're a go-getter," she said. "Another thing that attracted me to you right from the start. This guy wants to survive and doesn't wait around. Go for it, Elon. Isn't that what you say? Go for it?"

She then turned back to the table behind us.

"How would we enter this contest?" she asked the girl.

"Go to the owner. He's at the counter near the entrance. He wants to watch the singers and the crowd reaction to the singers from there."

Brigitte turned back toward me.

"You heard that, right?" she asked me.

I nodded yes.

"Let's go," she commanded. "If you're going to do

this, let's enter you now."

I felt emboldened with Brigitte in my corner.

"Are you the owner?" she asked a middle-aged man behind the checkout counter. As seemed to be natural to her, she took over the setting. "Do you speak English?"

"Yes," he replied in a serious tone. "Both questions, yes."

"My friend here is a singer from Texas. He speaks no Chinese but would like to enter your contest."

"He sings folk music? This is karaoke. He must sing from selections we have."

"He's a country singer from Texas. You know, like John Denver."

The owner lit up with a bright smile.

"He is like John Denver?"

Brigitte nodded yes.

"That would be good," the owner replied. "We have 'Take Me Home Country Roads' among our selections."

"I don't know that one," I said, interrupting.

"You don't have to know this song," the owner commented. "We have the words for you, and the music on a machine."

I shook my head no.

"I just need a guitar," I told him. "I'll sing you a Texas song and accompany myself on guitar."

The owner seemed prepared to say no, going by his disgruntled facial expression, but Brigitte intervened yet again.

"We come here all the time," she lied, "and your singers often have a guitar."

The owner pursed his lips, thought, then nodded.

"You have a guitar?" he asked.

"No," I answered. "I'd have to borrow one."

The owner grimaced, then smiled.

"Yes, we have a guitar for you. You can borrow and play while you sing."

We were in.

Shortly after we sat back down, the singing began. The arrangements on the karaoke seemed to make the singers stiff. Maybe they were unsure of themselves as singers, or perhaps from it being a canned arrangement.

"Oh, that was terrible," Brigitte groaned. "'Country Roads' is a hard song to sing anyway, I assume, going by the range and vitality required, but that guy was so out of his range. Gag." She looked at me reassuringly. "Glad you chose guitar and your own choice of what you want."

Two more singers also tried 'Country Roads' and it wasn't much better with them. The girl that tried had a broader range, but still struggled.

The accents hurt my ears. I was in their country and tried not to judge, but I was used to the original song in the original language. The Taiwanese not only had accents but often weren't sure of pronunciations.

"It's your turn, Elon," Brigitte said to me softly and calmly. She pointed at the owner. "He motioned for you to go. Good luck, mon cheri."

A young man met me at the stage, holding out a guitar. It was a small acoustical, but with an electric hookup to amplify the sound. The young man stayed to hold the microphone for me.

"Howdy," I said hoping to sound Texan. "I'm glad you speak English out there, because that's all I know. I won't do karaoke, but have an arrangement of a fellow

Texan's song. A famous guy back home named Bob Wills. He's inspired many people even today. I hope you like him, and me doing his song, my favorite song in the world, 'Faded Love.' It's a tear jerker. That's what we say if the song is a heartbreaker."

I strummed a G on the guitar and hoped it was tuned as the same key of G I played back home on my guitar. I looked out at them, ready to go. I felt nervous but excited. I was glad I was a Texan and hoped it differentiated me to the crowd.

The song lasted two minutes, but it seemed like two hours. Pure nothingness from the audience, as if floating inside a vacuum.

Brigitte wore a stark look on her face as I returned to our table.

"What the hell was that, Elon?" she moaned.

"The song or my performance?" I asked.

"Yes," she answered mockingly.

"A Texas song, 'Faded Love.'"

"Yes, you told us that. To be honest, I loved it. At least at first. I was shocked at how good your voice is. I thought we got this one locked up. A very soft and enamoring melody also. But the crowd just sucked all the energy out of the room. You should have sung Judy Collins or Bob Dylan if you wanted to sing sentimental. A bit more upbeat and something everyone has heard before. We blew our one shot."

I loved the way she used the word we. Us. Our partnership on everything. But the thought of blowing our one shot punched me in the gut.

"I'm going back up there," I said as I got up from my chair.

The next singer was on stage, but I went anyway. I

had to turn this around.

Brigitte watched me, then got up to talk to the owner, I assumed to explain things. The young man that handed me the guitar before was to the side of the stage, still with the guitar in hand. He looked at me, then the owner, saw the owner give a nod of approval, then came back on stage to hand me the guitar.

I had a "can't-miss" at the ready for them.

"'Big River,'" I said with a nod as my simple introduction for my reappearance. "Johnny Cash."

It worked. The crowd clapped in rhythm the entire time and gave me a standing ovation when I finished. I got pats on the back as I walked back to the table to Brigitte. The glint in her eye was an even bigger reward.

"Wow," she swooned. "What the hell was that?"

"Johnny Cash."

"Yes, yes, Elon, you told us that already. And I know Johnny Cash songs, but I never heard that one."

"Neither had the crowd. You have to be big on Johnny Cash to know this one. It was a big hit, but only in the country circles back home. It's got Luther Perkins pounding that guitar. He's Carl Perkins' brother."

"You had command, Elon, such command. You were in charge, *mi amor*."

I tried my best not to smile at her compliment, to look cool, calm and collected. But a smile came out anyway.

"The owner told me you could perform again after I explained to him why you chose the wrong song the first time, you being a foreigner and stupid and everything. He said he would give you another chance, but you were disqualified to win anything. He just decided to hear this upstart. He liked your voice and if you had a better song now, then he was game. He loved your 'Big River' as much as the crowd. He wants you to come in next week, he wasn't sure of the day, but has an hour open on Wednesday and said probably then. But somewhere next week you have your professional debut right here. Meaning he will pay you this next time. We've got to get you a guitar. You've got a lot of practicing to do, and then you and I will choose twenty songs for you to have at your fingertips. To sing at the drop of a hat. Right? The drop of a hat? A cowboy hat, if you like."

"I don't have money for a guitar," I reminded her.

"Use the guitar here for performances. But this is Taiwan. Somewhere they have a cheap guitar we can buy for you to practice with at my apartment. Our apartment, I mean. But don't get too excited. This is only the beginning. You are a nobody. An American nobody, but a nobody. I could only get you the equivalent of thirty dollars US for your first hour here. You get even that much because you are this long tall Texan. You better create a following, or you'll be stuck owing me forever."

She winked joyously, pride in me glowing from her as she did so. I had just broadened her horizons. She was now my musical manager. I wanted to kiss her right on the spot, in both affection and celebration.

Chapter 12

A restaurant one of my students had mentioned sounded interesting. It was lunchtime, and I had just finished a good workout in the gym. Brigitte was working, but that was good. I could check this restaurant to see if she might like it.

I rode my bicycle through the city and loved the hustle around me. I felt a part of Taipei by now.

We were getting the full brunt of summer, hot and humid, with no rain for relief. I was dripping in sweat by the time I arrived.

The restaurant had no air conditioning, though plenty of fans. It was roomy and clean, but not fancy. There was no a la carte service in this restaurant, nor even a buffet. Simply a few bins of steamed white rice, a small choice of vegetables, and several glass tanks of live black perch, each seemingly two pounds or more, going by their size. I was warned to bring someone with me because no one could possibly eat an entire fish. An entire fish must be bought, of course, since one could not kill half a fish.

I was from Texas, I encouraged myself, determined to eat the whole fish. Something inside still seemed indestructible.

"You not eat all fish," the owner of the restaurant warned me as I picked one out.

"I can do it," I said.

The man looked at me cynically, as if to say it was my funeral. He had my money already, so he walked away.

My belly felt full half way through the meal as my first doubts began to jeer at me. Excuses were already forming to compensate for my struggle to finish my mission. How thin I was after my hospital stay was the best one I came up with. Surely my stomach was now shrunken. But a wimp is a wimp, and that's what haunted me the most. No wimping out allowed. I continued onward.

It was pure drudgery to finish. I even ate my rice and vegetables. My time traveling the world made me self-conscious about wasting food, not just from wondering where my next meal was coming from at times, but all the hunger, even starvation, I had seen.

I felt self-conscious with my struggle to get out of my chair, followed by my waddle to the door. I hoped I didn't bump into anything. I was sure I would explode.

I couldn't get on my bicycle, much less ride it, so my waddle continued all the way back to the apartment while I pulled my bike beside me. I promised myself to never do this again.

No way was I bringing Brigitte to this restaurant. As much as I wanted to come back and eat like a civilized person, to enjoy a first-rate fish dinner, I knew she would eat a small portion only. Thus, I would be in nearly as bad a shape as now, if I brought her.

I collapsed on the bed when I arrived home. I had two hours to recuperate before my next class. Was I going to be able to get out of bed by then?

I still could not ride my bicycle as I made my way to work, but I brought it along, hoping I could ride it home. Somehow, I managed to teach the class. One of the students asked if I was sick.

"I worked out a little too hard this afternoon," I lied to them.

By the time I got home to Brigitte, I was my normal self. Even chipper.

"How was your day?" she greeted me while giving a polite and affectionate kiss. "Any big events for you today?"

"Seeing you again," I said as corny as I could sound, with even a glossy-eyed stare her way thrown in.

That got me another kiss. This one deeper. It was good to be home indeed.

"Would you like to go out?" she asked. "Have you eaten?"

"I'm not hungry. I had a good workout and am trying to lose weight."

"That is not a bad idea, Elon," she commented as she checked out my waistline. "It is good you got some of your weight back after your stay in the hospital. But slow down, perhaps. I see a midriff bulge appearing."

She looked at me with a snicker.

"Good word," she said. "Midriff bulge. I heard it on TV here. An American channel. Anyway, I did not notice your sudden midriff bulge until now. A bit bloated in the belly there. I must keep my stable of models slim and seductive, you know. Must I be this drill instructor person like in your Marine past?"

"Just more sex," I replied, straight-faced. "That'll take care of things. More sex and soon no more midriff bulge."

And all I had to do to prove it was to not go back to that restaurant again. Maybe things worked out after all.

Chapter 13

I was emboldened by the response to my first appearance at the folk house when I performed and won them over with "Big River." I knew not to sing ballads, but I still wasn't certain what the crowd would like. I was not going to sing "Country Roads," in spite of how much everyone loved that song. Even the bad renditions got some appreciation. I was sure I could do it better than anyone, but I resented how it seemed to be the only song people wanted to hear. Welcome to Texas, I swore to myself. I was going to open the hell out of their horizons.

I exuded confidence as I walked onto the stage for my professional debut the following Wednesday. My self-confidence surprised me, as a matter of fact. It was as if I belonged on stage. As part of some destiny.

I had twenty songs ready, and if one or two didn't work, I had plenty of others they would like. I would start off with the ones I considered can't-misses.

"San Antonio Rose" was my statement for my beginning. I was sure it would go over, and it indeed knocked them dead when I sang it, just like "Big River" had, or even more so. I felt a double satisfaction, since Bob Wills wrote this song, the same guy who wrote "Faded Love," the song that flopped on my audition.

After "San Antonio Rose," I tried another I was sure was its equal, a Hank Williams Gospel song. Hank was famous for "I Saw The Light," but "Are You Walking And A-Talking For The Lord" to me was even more piercing. It didn't matter if they understood what I was singing. The song itself was innervating with its energy and rhythm. I got yet another standing ovation. Some held up lit cigarette lighters as I sang.

The crowd was focused on me. I wasn't just entertaining them, I had them enthralled. As a singer I was as big a hit with the audience as the songs were for their quality. Song and singer were beyond a rapport. It satisfied me I could depend on these core songs, because I also wanted to experiment. If some song in my performance didn't work, I knew I had these to win back the audience. I would find more.

"They liked you," Brigitte greeted me as I met her at the door of the folk house to leave. She tokenly handed me my earnings, which I nudged back to her as a loan repayment. "The owner was smiling the whole time you sang." She gleamed. "He seemed enthused. You have a home here."

I couldn't hold back the smile of appreciation.

"He wants you back next Wednesday, stud. Do you like my Texas word? You are a stud, Monsieur. Another hour of singing for you coming up. Your singing career is not yet over."

I felt satisfied. Even snug. That mattered, not just for the money but for a sense of meaning in my stay in Taiwan. Because the next modeling show bored me yet again. I was sure that would happen. Now, after being a singer in a folk house, boredom from modeling seemed impossible to escape. A stark comparison and contrast. Texans do things like sing in a folk house. I wanted to repress my existence as a model.

The school was my steadiest income. But even then I still had to face Jean.

"I would like to take you to a place," she told me. "A beach. An hour drive from here. Is that fine with you? Not to swim. Just for the drive. There is a nice restaurant also. Then we can drive back. That will take most of the afternoon. Is it okay?"

"Sure," I said as I came to terms with the idea. "That would be nice. Thank you."

"You will enjoy. It is a very lovely drive."

Brigitte made ready to sneer as I told her of my latest offer from Jean, but she settled for reserved acceptance.

"I will have to draw a line somewhere," I told her. "I can feel it. But—"

"Enjoy yourself," Brigitte said matter-of-factly. "We haven't done any of this ourselves, and we've been together for a month now. What little time we have with each other didn't seem to warrant going off. But it is a small island. We could manage more." She looked up at me. "And we will. We will begin going to places ourselves, around the island. It is beautiful here, and I have a car. There is even a nice railway system here. They have the tallest mountain peak in eastern Asia, Mt. Alishan. Also a very nice lake in the narrow hinterland, called Sun Moon Lake. We're going to start doing these things. We're running out of time before your visa expires."

She broke into a grin while shaking her head.

"Another catalyst here," she said. "Jean pushes us into doing what we should have done on our own."

"It seems like I just got here," I said, trying to distract from the subject. "My visa will expire soon?"

"You didn't just get here, Elon. And in a couple of months you have to leave. Unless you go back to Mandarin classes and get a student visa again. Or unless you are okay with leaving instead."

She waited impatiently for a reply.

"What do you plan to do, Brigitte?" I asked. "Have you decided if you are staying or leaving Taiwan?"

She needed to think what to say. Irritation seemed building in her.

"Plan? What do I plan? I plan to punch you in the face. Answer me, Elon. What will you do? I'm already not in a good mood about Jean. Getting uglier by the minute."

"I'm happy here," I answered. "Even very happy."

"What about in a couple of months? You are so calm about your visa need. Why? Don't ask me about my plans. I am the one to ask that question about you. I have a visa. Soon you will not. Why is it of little concern to you?"

"I'll get a visa," I promised.

"You don't seem sure of yourself. Why are you not more sure of yourself? Why did I have to ask you?"

"I'm never sure of myself."

"That's the wrong answer," she said with a bite. "The wrong damn answer. God, I think I really am going to punch you in the face. Be more sure than that, Elon. Get some 'sure, I'm going to stay' in you damn quick. *Sacrement.*"

"Is that a cuss word?" I asked with a smirk. "You are cussing at me."

"I am glad you figure this out. That I am cussing at you. Damn you, Elon."

"Yes, I want to stay," I answered, showing guilt at

my unsureness. "Because of you. I like it enough to stay on my own, but I'm antsy to move on. It's my nature. But I want to stay with you. I want to stay because of you. I was never sure of our future. I just lived day by day."

"Why did you hurt me just now, Elon?"

I reached over to hug her, but she pushed me away.

"Damn you, Elon. Damn how much I love you. *Gottverdammt. Scheisse.*"

"That's not French."

"You know a bit of German if you lived in Bavaria last year," she noted. "I know you know these particular words. These are good, very, very good, German cursing words. German is so much better to curse with. *Scheisse, scheisse, scheisse.* So superior to *merde* for me."

She looked directly at my eyes to sneer.

"Can't you see I love you, Elon? You could leave me, though. Damn you for this."

I pushed my arms past her rejection and held on tightly while rubbing her neck.

"I love you too, Brigitte. I love you too. I really mean it. I'm sorry. We've been so happy. Unsure, but happy. Now it's time. We have to plan now. Yes. We do. Yes. I want to stay. I want to stay with you, and I'm so glad you want me to stay."

She gave a token push against me once more, then embraced me tenderly.

"Because of Jean we have now expressed our love," she said with a dreamy voice. "Is that not marvelous?"

She looked up at me chirpily.

"It took Jean and her car this weekend to prod us

into saying love for each other for the first time. Are we to be grateful to her, mon cheri?"

"Do you remember reading any Greek myths growing up?" I asked her with a chuckle. "How mischievous they were with their mortals, just for the fun of it, as if to relieve their tedium. Seems like Greek gods are in our lives and mischievous at our expense, bored with our happiness in the mundane. They like to liven things up for us."

She squeezed my hand.

"I hope they are happy," she said with a smile. "In spite of the frustrations, I am."

She looked at me apologetically while shaking her head.

"You did nothing wrong, Elon. We both have been living the day to day. I've known my feelings for you. I need signs of your feelings for me. Day to day is fine, but I also need reassurance. The need came out strongly now, beginning with Jean still wanting you. I have lived the day to day for emotional preservation. Unsureness. About your feelings and about mine. I am grateful to Jean now. We need her for this. For this about us. We are too complacent. I have felt love for you for so long, and here I am only now telling you. What if I told you and you did not answer with your own feelings that I need? Here we are. Professing our wonderful feelings."

Thank you, Jean, indeed.

Chapter 14

Jean drove us north of Taipei until we reached the coastline, then followed the national highway east until it veered southward. It was wonderful to see the ocean again. And this was the majestic Pacific Ocean. Some of the drive was on cliffs, with the slight elevation making an even lovelier impression as we looked down to the water. There were mountains in the distance, to add to the allure.

"We are a small country," Jean noted, "but Taiwan is a wonderful place to live. I spend most of my time in Taipei anyway, which is a large city. When I get out and drive, I soon run out of country, but it is big enough to have choices."

"Where we are now is a city," I corrected her.

"But not so big as Taipei, and we are on the edge of it. On the beach. The city is called Keelung City. Enjoy."

I still felt leery to encourage Jean, even if Brigitte weren't in my life. But I liked her more every time I was with her. I relaxed easily now around her and was grateful to her for the chance to get out and experience the Taiwan countryside, especially with a native-born Taiwanese.

"Elon," Jean said to me as we sipped our after-meal coffee at the seaside restaurant she chose. "I want to get us an apartment. For you. My father may get suspicious or protective of me if I lived with you. But you can move out of your dorm and live in a nice apartment and I can come see you there."

I was glad she thought I lived in my dorm. I flirted with letting her know my true living arrangement, since an apartment with her now would make her feel more possessive of me.

"Do you have such a large allowance?" I asked her.

"I work for my father. I make a good salary. I am not so important, so it is like an allowance. But I can afford, and I want to see more of you. You will enjoy the apartment."

"Don't get it yet, Jean," I pleaded. "I have paid rent already for a while. I have students come by sometimes for extra training. Thank you, though."

"Your students can see you in the apartment."

"The dorm is close to the school, and I like it," I replied. "And as I said, some of my students come to see me there. It would be awkward if you were in the apartment."

"I want to see you more. I can find an apartment near the school."

"Give me more time. Let me think about it. It is a nice offer."

She looked at me with disappointment.

"I hope soon, Elon. You are pleasant for me."

I could not make myself say anything to Brigitte about Jean's offer of the apartment when I arrived back home. Honesty was not the best policy, and I hated the Greek gods for this.

The telephone rang. Brigitte did little of the talking at first, but something exciting seemed to be happening, as her French grew more emotional during the conversation.

She hung up and walked briskly to me.

"My sister is getting married," she said gleefully as she sat down next to me. "Sometime this autumn, she said, but they haven't set a date. The date is waiting on me to see if I can go or not."

"Do you intend to go?" I asked.

"I must see," she replied. "It is sudden news, and to go half way around the world... It is a long time to be away from my work. I'm not sure I can arrange everything, and it is expensive also to go so far. So much time and effort. I must think."

"Do you know the guy she is marrying?"

"She marries a lawyer from Brussels. That is where they will live."

"A lawyer isn't going to want to run a farm," I commented. "Maybe he'll try to buy it from your dad, but I can't see him moving to your town and running a farm."

"Why are you thinking of this?" Brigitte inquired.

"Our conversation before. How there are just the two daughters in your family. Who will run your farm? Women make good managers, but it needs a man in the mix. Remember telling me all those things? So now what? Who will take over the farm, you know?"

"Why do you worry about this, Elon?"

"I just lost my farm. My parents did. I love farms. I was curious about yours, since you brought it up in our conversations."

"It is true. Perhaps my sister will never care about this farm of ours. I suppose that puts a pressure on me. I don't know yet these things. They will sort themselves."

She looked at me.

"You miss your farm?" she asked.

I nodded yes.

"What will you do then, Elon? After you leave here."

"I don't want to get into trouble with you again, Brigitte. I'm scared to answer that. I want my plans to include you, but we don't have plans yet. We live day to day. The phone call now with your sister has made me unsure about us. I feel this urgency thing we talked about before. Now it's an urgency about us too. I don't have so many new answers after all my travel, but I know I want to settle down someday. Now I think more about all that. Settling down, you know. I just don't want to be a robot while I'm doing it. I'm still not sure I'm up to what life has in store about settling down. I want things to teach my kids. Wisdom and knowledge things. Meaning I don't want to teach them things as much as how they can learn and grow and think with me. I'm still not up to that. You know, like what will I teach them if I don't know enough?"

"You are ranting, Elon. You have more thoughts than you have words, in your excitement. What are you talking about now? All this about the farm and your future. I don't follow all you are saying. Something is on your mind. How long will you stay here, then? Even after our anger and fight from this subject, you never said."

"I love you, Brigitte. We have a month and a half before I renew my visa. I'm still restless. But also I am happy here. So I planned to stay for another five-month visa stay and hope more falls into place. That's as far as I can see right now."

"Yes, we are happy," she concurred. "That's a good plan. I am happy too and feel important here. I have considered making Taiwan my home. But I know I will want to go home someday. And now there is the farm to consider. Yes, my father will want to know about the farm and its future. So I have much to consider. I am as doubtful as you."

Chapter 15

"Look, there is a nice-looking hotel," Brigitte said as we drove through a resort area partially up the slopes of Mt. Alishan, eastern Asia's highest peak. "And you can see the top from here." She looked at me in celebration. "Taiwan owns the highest peak in east Asia. That makes me proud. Let's check out the prices at this hotel. It looks clean."

It was surprisingly affordable, to my relief.

"What's to see?" I asked the girl behind the desk of the hotel as we checked in.

"You should take the Forest Railway," she replied with a broad smile. The smile seemed more than a courtesy for a guest. This girl seemed genuinely friendly.

"We have a car," I told her.

"Never mind that," the clerk answered. "Take the train. Let someone else drive you. The train goes through forests and tunnels. Just sit back and marvel."

"Do we have enough money?" I asked Brigitte, who read in her brochure.

She nodded her head. "The hotel clerk is right," Brigitte said. "The train is cheap. We can get cozy and just enjoy the ride and gawk while we do so. Gawk is a word, yes?" Brigitte asked with a tease. "We can marvel our life away for a few hours romantically."

"Yes," the clerk seconded. "It is very romantic."

"Are you from here?" I asked the girl.

"I am from this village. There is much work here because of people like you. Thank you for letting me stay in my own town with my wonderful job."

"So you want to spend your life here doing this?"

"Oh, no. I want to be a big shot. I want to be a manager someday."

"Aw, good. That's the spirit. But don't just think you can work your way up. Maybe so, but to manage a big hotel like this you have to be a good and knowledgeable business person. In particular, business for hotels."

"Perhaps," the girl said.

"No perhaps to it. Go to America. Study."

"I have no such money."

"Do it anyway. There's always a way."

"Americans are so optimistic. We are poor here."

"No, you're not. You're conquering the world now. America is taking notes from you. There is a college major in America at some universities called Hotel Management. Cornell is very expensive, but it is the best university for this. But there are others. Make it a goal. I want to come back here someday and see you in charge. Find a way to do this. You are from Taiwan. You can do anything."

"You want a free night in your room, I think," the girl said with a giggle.

"You just think about what I said. That's what's happening now. People like you from here and Japan or Korea or Singapore are studying in America."

"I still must charge you for your room," she said. "In spite of your advice and encouragement."

"Good. Good. You're going to go far. Good luck."

"Good luck to you, kind sir. Enjoy your time with us."

"What was that about?" Brigitte asked me affectionately while grabbing my hand to hold as we walked to the nearby train station.

"Education is so underrated," I answered. "Enough kids go to college to party and enough schools take your money that sometimes it seems a waste, a formality only. A check on some to-do list rather than learning things. Book things, but things. I loved going to college. Not just the college life, but there was a whole new world there. History, science, literature. I couldn't believe how much you can learn from books."

"So you travel the world to do this learning."

"That too, Brigitte. Education any way you can get it. Street wise, book wise. Both send chills up my spine. Backpacking is underrated, too, since you brought it up. Education, period, is underrated."

"I never met anyone like you, mon cheri."

"That's why we're holding hands, ready to ride a train together."

She nodded approvingly.

Because we had no reservations, we had to ride in a cattle car on the train. Meaning no seats for us. The wide door was open and the view was broad for us to easily take in. Hills were abundant around us, and soon a forest appeared, just as we had heard. Finally we reached the end of the line and were greeted by a large Buddhist temple.

"The name of this temple is the Shoujhen Temple," Brigitte informed as she read from her travel guide. "If we go up to the second floor, there are ten thousand Buddha statues. And it has many priests."

Chinese architecture mixed with Japanese was abundant. Both of these empires once ruled Taiwan. Buddhist religious paraphernalia was throughout the temple.

"I love Buddhist temples," I said in reverence. "Let's talk to a priest. They are all around in the temple."

"Let's eat first," Brigitte suggested. "There are so many places from which to choose. We will eat and come back and find a priest for us. I'm hungry, but also just to savor some food in this place. Part of being a tourist. First the body, then the soul."

"What does your guide say about food here?"

"To eat it," she said with a laugh. "There is a type of pancake, also a broth, a type of sausage—"

"That's the magic word," I interrupted. "Let's get a sausage."

As we walked back outside we noticed a post office.

"Look," Brigitte said, pointing. "Look there across from us."

She increased her pace, leaving me slightly behind.

"These are postcards," she noted while holding one up to inspect. "Made out of wood. That's marvelous. Let's send to everyone we know. Family anyway. Make them jealous. We are here. We are in exotic paradise and you are stuck in the mundane."

"So much for the body," I teased her. "The soul is louder after all."

After buying our wooden postcards, we found the sausages we wanted, which were prevalent in the many small restaurants throughout the village. Even the street vendors had them.

"Oh, man," I swooned. "A sausage is a sausage, but somehow the Chinese do it better. I wonder what kind of spices they add. I can't place it."

"Maybe ginger," she said. "There's so many spices in this part of the world."

"I still want to talk to a priest," I said as we ate.

After we finished eating, I approached the lady vendor who had sold us the sausage.

"Speak English?" I asked her.

"Little English," she replied. "Television."

"Are you Buddhist?"

"Yes, Buddhist."

"The temple here has many priests. Will they talk to us?"

"Why talk priest?" she asked quizzically.

"To learn about Buddhism."

"Many priests here. What you want talk? I am Buddhist. I talk to you."

"Can you give instruction on Buddhism? Lessons?"

"Buddhist is Buddhist. Like Christian. Love. Peace. Eat sausage. Work."

Brigitte and I let out a laugh. I grabbed the lady's hand to shake it in appreciation of how earthy she was. She spoke well about Buddhism, for sure.

"Yeah," I said to Brigitte as we walked away. "People are people. They live their lives. There are differences, I'm sure, but mostly we are the same damn clay. Life has meaning or not."

"Such a philosopher," she said with a laugh. "That is enough talk for today, for certain. Let's just go around and enjoy. We'll see a priest at a less busy time."

The ride back down to our hotel was like re-watching a good movie. The same thrills occurred except with greater detail.

"Let's have a real meal," I suggested once we arrived back in our village. "There are so many restaurants. We'll walk around until we find something that grabs us."

It seemed an excuse to see more of the village as we walked. The peak of the mountain still flirted in the distance.

"There's one with a television," Brigitte said, looking at a restaurant across an alleyway in front of us. "I would like to see some news. We've been out of the loop."

Instead of news, however, they showed a replay of Elvis Presley's last concert. We sat at a table and watched.

"Elvis, somehow," I commented, "is the universal language."

When our orders arrived, we continued to watch as we ate. Brigitte seemed to have only minimal interest, barely a curiosity, but I was engrossed. Elvis brought back so many memories.

Toward the end, he sang gospel songs with his Southern gospel backup groups. The songs moved me, and I slumped, with intense focus, as I watched. Brigitte studied me uneasily and some of the near tables looked at me in disgust.

I was silent on our walk back to our hotel.

"Are you such an Elvis fan?" Brigitte asked finally, when we arrived at our room.

I nodded that I was.

"Everyone thought you ready to cry while we were

watching."

"I know I looked like a groupie," I replied, embarrassed.

"You did."

I turned to her for emphasis.

"Whenever I hear the passage, 'What good is it for someone to gain the whole world, yet lose their soul,' I think of Elvis."

I hesitated, to collect my thoughts.

"Not that I think he's evil and in hell. But Elvis got so trapped being Elvis. 'Imprisoned' is probably a better word. He really seemed such a good person. Deep, even. You can't tell from the movies and concerts. He gained godlike fame and then lost his mother almost in one breath. Lost his bearings. He seemed to want more than being *Elvis*, just looking at him like tonight on TV. That's what I was thinking as I watched. How lost he looked. How sad it made me. All those things he learned growing up that moved him. Huge spirituality. Not just religion, but that too. So much got pushed to the side after he became godlike, and he couldn't seem to find the real and human him anymore. I believe he was looking. He was too stuck in living out his Elvis movies, though. He was still creative, but he lost so much of even that."

"That's what caused your mesmerized focus while we watched the television?" she asked, amazed.

"Yeah. I hurt for him. He was so phony during most of the concert. And then from what link he still had with God and the real Elvis in him, so many memories of better and deeper things in him came to me. When he sang 'How Great Thou Art,' he seemed desperate, to me. Like 'help me.' I didn't even like the way he performed the song. Still too much show for me. But that hunger was still there to see inside him. Maybe I put it there in my mind, but I'm sure I saw a lost soul wanting out somehow."

"All that from watching a television special," she responded. "I never cared until now. I just saw the fat old phony. The has-been."

"All the sadder," I answered. "He was the most underrated and overrated singer at the same time."

"You are a strange one." She sighed. "We don't really have talks like this. I expected more of them from you, the way you seemed to me when I met you. You have been living a new adventure most of our relationship, this one a Taiwan adventure with a glamorous movie star. Ha. Me, you know. Say yes, okay? But I'm glad now we saw Elvis tonight. I like this in you."

She looked at me wistfully. "I hope this begins another phase for us," she said. "I want more of this Elon and the me that comes out from it."

She laid her head on my shoulder while clutching her arms around me.

"Talk to me, Elon. I want to know you. Really know you. Lay it on me. Give me the deeper Elon. What is ticking there inside of you?"

"Are you sure?" I asked. "I think all kinds of things around you but am afraid of boring you or looking weird."

"We are here at this wonderful place," she answered. "This is special, and I am in the mood for this Elon now. This will be our Buddhist moment since we just came from the temple before. No priest except ourselves now. Buddhism as life, I suppose I am trying to say. Philosophy, the soul. Life, like the vendor lady suggested."

I thought where to begin.

"It's natural to question in our teens," I said. "Part of growing up. Religion and the Bible moved me, but I was already questioning things about evolution and hell in my adolescence. Questioning in ways my church didn't like. Then one day a bully messed with me when I was in high school. He was bigger than me, and that mattered. If I had been twice his size I could have shaken him off. Even endured a slap or two, and me and my religious friends might have admired my restraint and generosity. But this bully guy could have kicked my ass. While all this was happening, I remembered things the Bible said. You know, turn the other cheek. So I stood there stoically like I knew I should. And he slapped me again and mocked me as a coward. Instead of feeling above him or enlightened, I was humiliated. Instead of loving my enemy, I hated him for it."

"That's natural," Brigitte comforted. "We are never up to our ideals."

"But the humiliation was deep," I continued. "Like I fell into some abyss and void. It occurred to me how turning the cheek did not mean to feel humiliation like I felt. I was not strong enough at all to be up to this supposed virtue. I was not wise and loving, and I needed that to be what is meant of us. I hated the guy that mocked me. I just couldn't do anything about it. I couldn't defend myself by kicking his ass like I wanted, or exude any love and grandeur toward him and change him for the better. It takes love to exude love. Not metaphors. My religion did not prepare me up to this point. I'm not blaming religion. I'm blaming my approach."

"You took the Bible literally, you mean," Brigitte surmised. "It was a law to you instead of a virtue."

"Exactly, Brigitte. It was good that I didn't lose faith in the Bible after the bully incident. My learning instincts knew there was truth in the Bible. The humiliation, however, showed me something in my search was missing, and drastically. Huge. I had to let go of some of this literalness in me and find more meaning. More than I found before. I was taught there was only one way and to follow the one path. There may be an ultimate path, but restricting the search to a path I understood little about is not the way to find that path. Faith is great, but blind faith sucks. In spite of whatever I got out of the Bible, something was missing. I felt I should rebel a bit. That's what teenagers are good at anyway. I figured I'd better get with it. Live in chaos more, to loosen up my straight and narrow."

"Yes," she agreed. "So teenagers act wild. Life lessons. A bridge to adulthood."

"But people lose their way doing that, too," I countered. "I knew so many people that lost their way, in fact. Rebellion is not enough. Keep your head clear and feet on the ground while you do it. Don't just rebel. It's as shallow as believing things literally. Especially when we're young and inexperienced. The warnings we hear about rebellion are true. How one easily gets swayed following some idea or false god. So even with my questioning I wanted to be slow and deliberate with these questions. Be careful. Let the buyer beware. I didn't want to be a wild teenage punk."

"We are only mortals, Elon. God is the infinite. We

will never be God."

"But Brigitte, I was leap years behind even for a mortal. So much was over my head. Not just my intellect, but my inner soul. How do you open up and also not get trapped by every false god and hope while you're abandoning so many beliefs and rules? You end up trading religion for a cult or drugs or a charismatic figure, or materialism. It's scary business, looking for truths you don't know, but I needed answers."

"We need our rules," Brigitte added, "but yes, someday, as we mature, we need to go beyond the restrictions. To seek for more."

"I am a natural seeker," I continued. "I was when I accepted things more literally, too. Seeking is inherent in me, very strongly. But once I ventured out more, it was like a genie let out of the bottle. There's no going back. My emotions are so strong. Ruthless. They won't let me be a John Wayne, or a Beatle, or any one aspect I admire. I can be anything up to a point, but something pushes so strongly in me to go beyond. Always beyond. More, more, more. Everything seems confining after a while, if we don't keep growing. What did Bob Dylan say? Something like if we're not busy living then we're busy dying. I could end up with a nervous breakdown if that is what it takes to break boundaries. To go further out in the arena. It's like there are tectonic plates inside me."

"What do you mean tectonic plates?" she asked.

"Like the San Andreas Fault in California. Somewhere the geological layers and plates underground shift under pressure. Mountains form, earthquakes happen, volcanoes erupt and such when this shifting takes place. Don't dream of building a house there, at whatever maturity level, because there's going to be an earthquake inside me someday if I don't continue on in my search. I'll have to find a new place to go."

"So that's when you started traveling? As part of the search?"

"Not immediately. I had to get some bearings about my chaos first. All this questioning our generation and the times did in the sixties made sense to me. Except that our generation had only let out the genie and didn't know anymore than I did about what to do with it. So travel became a part of it for me, finally. To get out, to be disoriented. I used to call them agility drills. To have to adjust and grow and squirm to survive. To see things and experience them and keep from getting killed or screwing up beyond repair."

"And so here we are," Brigitte said soulfully. "I didn't have such an epiphany, but here we are. Searching together. Questing and questioning together now."

"Here we are in Taiwan," I concurred. "You and me. Like some cosmic link."

"Yes," she said, nodding, "like some cosmic plot."

"Here we are in one of the developing Asian tigers. How fitting. Taking it all in with how determined they are, and focused, while we marvel at the whys of how they are this way and how they are right for it. Not materialistic as much as feet on the ground while pulling themselves out of a hole."

"That too, Elon. You are right. Don't apologize for the material needs of life. But materialism shouldn't absorb us. We can lose our way with the spiritual or the mundane or anything else. But material things have their place in the perspective of life. Practical things. Common sense things."

"It's so damn complicated, Brigitte. But I need all this. I'm desperate for it. Yes, even the material has its place, but not as an excuse to overshadow the spiritual. I'm still looking for all these spiritual Easter eggs. I hope it's a phase. Will I ever have a life?"

"We'll have it together," she said. "I love our talks, Elon. We must have more."

Chapter 16

"We need more songs," Brigitte cheerfully told me after my performance for the night at the folk house. "The manager is very happy. You're a hit, babes. You knew that by the audience, but it is official now. You get another hour. He is asking if you prefer a two-hour performance or two one-hour slots."

"Probably better to do a two-hour, don't you think? You may have a modeling show that conflicts. That already happened once."

"That is what I think also. Yes, one two-hour is better than two one-hour shows. Either way, you need more songs so you don't sound— What is this word?"

"Redundant," I said to help out.

"Yes, yes. I know this word. Redundant. You don't want to sound redundant."

"They even liked my ballad," I bragged.

"What ballad?" she asked.

"'Detroit City.'"

"That's not a ballad. You put a rhythm to it. It is very melodious indeed. But yes, another song they like. Keep experimenting."

"I even got a standing ovation on that one."

"It is melodious. Find other ones like that. Melodious but with some rhythm."

I looked at her in celebration as we got up to leave. We didn't hang around after performances anymore. I got too much attention.

"This is fun," I said to Brigitte as we left the folk house. "I could stay here another five months, for sure."

"In a month you must reapply for your school visa, then."

I nodded. My mind swirled at how everything seemed to be falling into place.

"As I watched you perform tonight," Brigitte noted, "then talked to the owner about you and about the extra hour he's giving you, I had to wonder about you. Here we are, half way around the world, in our twenties. I know how I ended up a model and then in charge, but you—you are such a natural singer and performer. What took you so long to start singing professionally?"

"I met you," I replied.

She shook her head.

"No, Elon, no. Not that. I am not the answer to this riddle. A catalyst perhaps, but not the reason you started so late. If you had this dream for so long, why did you need a catalyst like me? What kept you?"

"I'm a shy person."

"Ahh. You shy? I see it in you some, but no. That isn't what happened."

"Did you see Joe Cool?" I asked, showing disgust at his memory. "What an idiot he was? Even if he had the people going, he's an idiot. I met so many Joe Cools in my life. With even less ability than he has. He at least got a routine going. Got out in the arena and found something to work with. I've met people who were almost tone deaf and they convinced themselves they were good singers. I wanted what they did. You know, the attention, and the sharing of songs I love. But I was scared I was as screwed up as they were. That I would just talk myself into thinking I was good when I was a goon instead."

"But you're not a goon singer. You couldn't tell the difference?"

I shook my head no.

"So many people I've known were convinced they were Joe Cool," I emphasized again. "Why would I have been different from them? I ended up in my younger years sure I wasn't good, just wanting to believe I was."

"But you are different, Elon. You are so different. So talented. Not a Joe Cool at all. Shame on you for your worries about such things."

"I don't know what to tell you, Brigitte. It took a long time to figure it out. There were a few people, through the years, who heard me sing and made me think maybe I was talented. That I wasn't just another Joe Cool. And then I met you. By then I didn't care. I was going to make it anyway. For you."

Brigitte swooned as I spoke. She gripped my hand tightly.

****

But there was still Jean.

"I would like to take you for the weekend," she said to me one day.

"You mean the entire weekend? Away the whole time?"

"Yes. There is a very lovely place on the southern tip of Taiwan. It is called Kenting Town. Maybe we don't go to the town itself. Nearby are resort areas. There are beaches, including with coral reefs, and also there are some mountains in the area. It is all very lovely. You will enjoy. But we should do more than just drive and return. So we must spend the weekend."

"That is so nice of you, Jean. But I don't think I can be away an entire weekend. I have things I must do."

"What must you do? May I help? Surely, there is a weekend you can get away."

"Yes, I probably can. But I'm not sure I can. I can't explain everything I do, but sometimes other students invite me to a temple or church or an opera."

"Oh, you like the opera? We can go to the opera if you like."

"Sure. But let me arrange a weekend for Kenting Town. I'll let you know."

"Please this, Elon. Thank you. I will look forward."

I knew I'd better tell Brigitte about this new event, plus finally include Jean's desire to get me an apartment.

"You are going to shack up with her?" Brigitte shrieked. "That is what you say, right? She wants this from you? This word, shack up. A sex orgy arrangement?"

"I'm not going to do this, Brigitte. I already told you that. Please don't make me regret I told you. Help me out here. How am I going to handle all this with Jean?"

"Have a sex orgy, for sure. That is how I would handle it. You know that."

"Brigitte, I will break my relationship with her, if that's what you want, but I wanted to talk it over first and see what you could figure out."

"I figured out sex orgies are very appealing," she spit back.

I wanted to laugh except I was scared to death.

"Let me play her along just a bit longer," I pleaded. "In a couple of weeks my visa runs out. Maybe I'll just get the hell out of here."

Brigitte's snarl increased.

"Not without you," I added.

"Was I going somewhere?" she returned.

"Let me appeal to the school owner, Mr. Chu. Maybe he'll understand what a mess I'm in and take pity on me."

Brigitte suddenly seemed to deflate.

"I'm sorry," she said showing her frustration. "I am still so possessive. I do believe you want a relationship with me and that you feel on a spot with this Jean girl. I'm sorry. I wasn't being fair to you. My God, what's our marriage going to be like? Am I going to look at my watch every minute you are late home?"

I stared at her and hoped she understood why I was doing so.

"So, are you going to marry me or not?" she asked.

"Let me talk," I pleaded. "Before you scream. I love the thought of getting married to you."

"But—" she said mockingly. "There is a 'but' somehow."

"How are we going to do it, Brigitte? All this is so fast and so new to me. I don't want you to think I don't need you. But I'm coming from a different place about it. All this disorients me. But I want to marry you. Absolutely. Let's do that. Get married. But how are we going to do this?"

"Get your new visa, and I will check things out," she answered with confidence. "I'm a permanent resident here. It can be arranged. Getting married is new to me also, but now I know I want it. Adjust to it, my dear. We're going to do it. So adjust. You'll love the idea."

"Are we going to live here? I love it here, but suddenly this is to be my home?"

"It is all complicated, isn't it, mon cheri? Ahh, this silly Jean girl. But we were going to get married anyway, and you know it. Probably soon. So thank you, brat Jean. *Merde*. I suppose I am happy. I am, but yes, these decisions all of a sudden! We will be married, Elon. Enough anxiety over this happy event."

"Okay, let me talk to my boss at the school first, though," I cautioned. "If I get married, she is going to quit. Let me explain things to him. I feel badly for him."

Brigitte walked over to me to kiss me. I hugged her and kissed her back. It was a crazy world I lived in, but it seemed to fit my style.

"Is Jean one of these crazy Greek gods you mentioned?" Brigitte asked. "Or just the messenger?"

Chapter 17

I loved the feeling after a good run. I was up to six miles and ran it regularly. I thought back to my Marine buddies and how some claimed they loved the run itself. I felt a pride while I was running, but I did not enjoy the run while I was physically doing it, or the weightlifting as I did that. It was pure discipline with me to do these workouts. I felt marvelous afterwards, however, as my body worked on recovery.

The hot, humid Taiwanese summer was taking its toll on me as I did my workouts. I had endured such weather while growing up in South Texas by the Gulf of Mexico, so I was used to it. But a rash formed now at my thighs and was getting worse by the day. I determined the problem was the tight, thick polyester bathing suit I wore over my cotton underwear. There was nowhere for my sweat to go.

"You are so red in the face, Elon," Brigitte said sympathetically as she wiped at me with a towel. "How was your run? You look in pain. Is it your rash?"

I pulled up the right thigh area of my swimsuit to show her.

"It is so much worse even since yesterday, Elon. You must see a doctor."

"I'm not going to a doctor," I snapped back.

"So then," she said with a bite, "I must bully you. You are indeed going to a doctor. We are to be married soon, and I want a honeymoon. So if you are crazy, I am not. For my own sake, you are going to a doctor."

"I have a balm. I'll rub some on the rashes. It's good for that."

She shook her head skeptically.

"It is more than a rash now," she said while she inspected my thigh more thoroughly. "See these spots and lines inside the rash? That is fungus. You are growing fungus on your thighs now. I should have seen how this was getting, but usually it is in the dark when we spend time exposed. A balm will not fix this mess growing on your thigh. You must see a doctor."

"For what?" I whined. "He'll look at it and give me a potion to put on it. I'll get my own potion."

She thought for a moment.

"You go shower," she instructed. "I will be back quickly."

I inspected both my thighs under the overhead light just before I entered the shower. The rash had grown substantially overnight, and just like Brigitte said, there was some kind of growth in it, too. This grossed me out, thinking about a parasitic fungus going after my thighs.

The shower felt soothing as it relaxed my stiff and fatigued muscles. It stung my thighs at first, before the warm moisture softened and comforted the area in turmoil.

By the time I dried myself with a towel, Brigitte was back.

"Just stay in your birthday suit," she told me. "I have the solution."

I looked at her to see what she had in her hand.

"Come to the bed," she instructed. "You need to lie

down so you can rub this all over your thighs. The rash goes down to your buttock area."

"Rub what?" I asked her curiously.

"Come to bed. I'll show you."

I lay down on our bed as she pulled out a small jar from her purse and sat next to me at my feet.

"That's a balm," I sneered in irritation. "I already had one."

She shook her head and let out a wicked laugh.

"No, my dear. This is not a balm. This is *the* balm. This is Tiger Balm. It is so strong it is outlawed in America and Europe. Your fungus will regret the day it intruded on your lovely thighs."

She handed the jar to me. I inspected it. It looked like any other balm to me.

I unscrewed the lid and immediately the strong aroma hit me squarely in the face. It wasn't just the odor, an odor similar to balms I had used before. These fumes made an impact; they were a force on my skin. My nostrils quivered, while the skin on my face seemed to flinch. I looked at her for a clue of some sort. She simply stared in anticipation, as if waiting for the show.

I pulled out a glump with my right index finger and began rubbing it into my rashes. Before I finished rubbing, I began to feel the onslaught the balm was making. I didn't mind a bit of pain, however. It seemed a good sign.

"Be very careful not to get any of this balm on your jewels, my sweet. We will want to make love again."

I made ready to laugh at her analogy, but suddenly felt increased pain—a pain similar to a laceration. The realization of her little joke was taking place. By the time I finished rubbing it all in, the full thrust of the balm's power devoured me.

"My God," I howled. "My God."

In agony, I buckled my knees and spread them as widely as I could.

"Oh, my God," I howled more. "Brigitte, help me."

With that, she walked to the table, where an electric fan was placed. She turned it on and pointed it directly onto my thighs, as if they were on fire and the cool air an extinguisher. It helped.

"You will be fine by our honeymoon," she said with a giggle. "Even sooner. But tonight we cannot make love."

She looked at me wickedly as I banged the bed with my fists while sneering at her. Her amusement infuriated me further.

"You did this on purpose, Brigitte," I said angrily.

"It will get rid of your fungus and rash. We will buy you better shorts and not deal with this greenhouse your bathing suit created on your garden area. Next time you will prefer a doctor. You see, I am the perfect bully. Do you still want to marry me?"

As much as I was in pain, and as much as I hated her just now, I let out a laugh of my own.

"After I kill you," I said with my arms and hands outstretched as if to choke her. "Then I'm going to kiss you and someday we're going to make love like we never have before. But for now, leave me to my torture."

Chapter 18

"We don't want to see all the scenes in Taiwan now and have nowhere to go for our honeymoon," Brigitte commented as she drove.

"Well, isn't Sun Moon Lake like the biggest tourist attraction?" I asked.

"Maybe. Probably. There are many good places. Including this place down south Jean wanted to take you, Kenting Town. Maybe that is where we'll spend our honeymoon, except it would be some irony to do that, since Jean has claimed title to this idea for you. But I want to go to Sun Moon Lake now. Just to make sure we see it. Your visa runs out next week, and what if the worst happens? I want to see this with you. I have never been there myself and always wanted to go, so I am glad for the both of us we can see it now."

"And it's in the mountains, too?"

She nodded yes.

"It is their biggest lake," she noted, "something like five square kilometers. I don't know what in miles."

"Almost two," I informed.

"That is a nice size," she commented, "and it is a fourth of the way up in altitude as Mt. Alishan. Meaning as high as the village where we stayed at Mt. Alishan. There is a cultural village by the lake also, and another temple. Maybe this time we will really talk to a priest and not a noodle vendor, ha. Whatever we have time for or are in the mood for."

"Maybe we'll come back for our honeymoon," I said joyfully.

She looked over at me and smiled.

"So Jean is no concern now?" Brigitte asked. "Your school owner understands?"

"He wasn't happy I have problems with her, but he knew I probably would be leaving soon anyway, so he was settled with the idea that she may not be his client for much longer, if I finally start saying no to her advances. He was happy I am renewing my visa and will stay more. That helped compensate, and I will hang on to Jean a little longer. Until it comes to a head again."

"Or until we get married. Whichever comes first."

"Yeah. That. Either way, it will be uncomfortable when he loses her as a student."

"Why do you worry so about her, Elon? She is a rich spoiled brat. Welcome to the cruel world."

"I like her, Brigitte. And she's so young. I know it's a life lesson for her and all. I don't lose sleep, but I don't relish hurting her. She's really a sweet girl."

Brigitte looked over at me as if considering what I just said.

"Okay," she replied as if relenting. "I am not cruel, but she bothers me. She will be a better person to know she didn't get something she wanted so much. Meaning you. Meaning damn you. You did not lead her on. String her along is the better word, I suppose. She pushed this situation on you. Not you on her. Just get your visa and we will do what we must."

The subject put us in an awkward mood. We

remained silent the rest of the drive.

"Hey," I chirped as we entered the village. "Do you see that bed and breakfast up ahead? It looks clean on the outside, and sturdy. Let's give it a look."

"Yes," Brigitte seconded. "This is a good spot. Forests are nearby." She looked at me approvingly. "This is perfect for a honeymoon. We must consider coming back then. Even if we see all we hope to see now. We must consider coming back for our honeymoon, to live out the best parts of it."

This idea put us in a good mood as we checked into our cozy room with a nice double bed. There was a good view of the forest from a side window.

"Footpaths," Brigitte said as she pointed in the distance. She looked at me, smiling. "There are footpaths to walk. Maybe to the lake. We will find this out. Even if they don't go to the lake, it will be a refreshment for us."

"First," I interrupted, "let's check out the temple. I love temples."

This temple was quaint and small compared to many we had seen up to now. We browsed through it for the serenity.

"I can't believe it," I said pointing to the far corner. "A priest. We actually get to talk to a priest. I had hoped, but almost quit believing."

We walked to him, but he seemed oblivious to us until just before we were on him. I nodded politely as a greeting.

"We would like to talk to you," I said.

He stared at us.

"Do you have a moment to talk to us about Buddhism?" I asked him.

"No English," he replied stoically. "I no English."

I had to make myself smile from my frustration. He made a slight smile back at us before walking away. I looked at Brigitte while shrugging my shoulders.

"Just to know we talked to a priest would have been nice," I said.

"We did," Brigitte corrected. "Technically we did. Then he told us he no speaky. So no matter. We will buy a book."

"I've already read books on Buddhism."

"We'll buy one here. Just for the sake of it. As the British say, we must have a stiff upper lip. No priest, we'll manage, but a book at least."

I let it go, then looked at her with an idea.

"To compensate," I said, "if we can't talk to a priest, then let's have a meditation. Here's a temple. Let's meditate in it. Who needs a priest when we have God?"

We chose a corner of the temple next to a small Buddha statue for our meditation, a token Buddhist element for our endeavor.

"I meditate without crossing my legs," I informed Brigitte. "You've seen pictures of the lotus position, I'm sure. I used to meditate with a religious study group, and we just sat upright with our feet squarely on the floor."

"That sounds more natural," she responded. "At least until I understand this lotus position and how to do it correctly."

We sat silently with eyes closed for a few minutes, then walked silently out of the temple.

"Any deep discussions for us, my dear?" Brigitte asked playfully while we lay snuggled later that night at

Sun Moon Lake. "Does the surrounding forest and lake bring out anything inside of you? Or the temple today? We didn't stay long, but did it stir anything in your deepest soul?"

"I am in a mellow mood because of all these things, but I don't feel so philosophical right now. I'm glad. I like getting away. This is away. I want to wallow in it. Peace of mind."

"I feel philosophical, if you don't mind," she said. "I'm glad you chose to meditate today in the temple. I did it once at my university. At a cultural seminar we had. I didn't get anything out of it. Religiously, anyway. I am sure it helps relax you, but it didn't draw me to it. You know, make me want to do it. But I enjoyed it today in the temple with you. In its own environment."

"I used to meditate regularly," I said. "I told you. With that study group. I still sometimes do, somewhere, when I'm in the mood. I never really got into it myself, but I used to go to a study group while I was in college, a religious and philosophical one, like I said. We began and ended with meditation. I do it as a peaceful memory more than I get anything out of it in itself. And I just wanted to pay respect to my past with it here. Like you say, in its environment."

"So thank you for that, Elon. But now, what I really want to talk about is more down to earth. About us, in particular. We must think of what we want. I mean really want. In our future together, I mean. It is good to stay in such a wonderful country for us. We are perfect here for now. Especially as we get out into the countryside and the culture more. I was living day by day with little thought about anything until you came. I am not making definite plans, but now I feel myself wanting plans. I want a home with you. With children. If we have children, then I cannot work. Perhaps I can. I am a manager now more than a model. I like the extra money of being a model, but it is not that much for the little modeling I do now. I don't know when we will have children, but I want them soon. And I cannot be sure if I can be a manager then. You cannot afford a family by yourself. We still have time. I mean there is no rush for children, but I still think about it. I have more to think about now, and I want to think about it."

She looked over at me.

"And what about you, my sweet? What thoughts do you have on this, Elon? You were going to go home and see about settling down, until you met me. Then you are staying. But we are not in a permanent way here. So what are your thoughts?"

"I have a college degree," I replied. "I've worked professionally. That's when I felt so trapped. In some cage. It will be different now, but I am nervous about it. I had to adjust to you, and you are a joy. I have to adjust to a permanent job soon."

"It's normal to be nervous," she comforted.

"We're half way around the world. That's a more nervous situation. There is this underlying feeling that it's all settled somehow, though. As if we'll find out about it soon. It's good to think about settling down, but somehow it's already planned. Maybe that's just my way of not getting hyper about things."

"A fatalist," she said as she rubbed the bridge of my nose. "A romantic one, however. Myself also. I am a romantic and a fatalist. I am nervous, but only a bit. I have been on my own for so long now. We are only able to deal with the present and the immediate future. The rest we just don't know yet. I have faith in myself and in my future. And now you are in my life. At first I thought to settle here or perhaps go home, my two biggest ideas. Or even to go to Hollywood and seek my fortune there. Before now, these were far-off thoughts to me. A tease. Then you enter. Was I expecting you? Like some Prince Charming, maybe? But here you are. As if all planned. Something is planned for us, Elon. I agree with you about that. It is our duty to consider our lives and our future, but something is waiting for us. We must be alert and aware, but some wheel is turning, I think. It is planned, yet left to us to fulfill. To be worthy of our destiny."

I stared off to absorb her thoughts and wallow in the cozy feeling of how the great cosmos was in on this. Were such notions intuitive or just part of our security needs? Or just some superstition? I had no idea, but it was fun to deal with all these thoughts about us. It made Brigitte and me more at one with each other, now that we were doing it together. I liked that. Maybe that was the purpose of thinking about it all. We had nothing left to do but get married and ride the waves with our circumstances.

Brigitte placed her hand on my chest.

"So here is Elon in a transition," she said, just above a whisper. "You are a romantic. Romantic about life, but also about women. You were no virgin when we met. You have not only experienced life, but you love women. Me especially. So I keep wondering why you did not get married before. Even if you were a confused but independent guy. You were when we met, also, and look at us now. Why are you so available?

You love women too much to still be single this long in your life. You will be thirty in a few years. I haven't seen your dealings with women, not even with Jean, but there is this vibration in you, and it attracts women. Even that young clerk at the hotel at Mt. Alishan. The caring you do so easily, especially with women."

"I love women, yeah. I hate to put it that way because it usually means some playboy type. Some cad or happy-go-lucky jerk that goes for it. But I've always loved women. Women are precious. Special. Innocent until proven guilty. There is something so spiritual about women. It is irresistible to me."

"That's my point, Elon. I haven't seen you with women so much, but I see this about you. I feel it too while experiencing being the love of your life. So why did you never fall in love and marry some love of your life before me? Not counting the great cosmos had better plans for you. Meaning me."

The memories flowed as I listened to Brigitte describe this side of me. Indeed, why wasn't I married by now? With all the encounters I had while growing up…

"When I was preschool," I began as I thought back, "I was stuck on the farm, except for church. They put us in Sunday School with kids our age. I always sat by girls. They were so sweet. I mean…I was drawn to them. I didn't think about it at the time. I didn't know I was supposed to be too young for girls. I was even too young for supposed puppy love."

"What is puppy love? I hear this term and think I know. What is it exactly?"

"Like affection, but not so deep. Like for a puppy dog. As if the hormones are starting to wake up, but not the full impact. But I can tell you I fell in love, deeply in love, with this little girl back then."

I saw Brigitte raise her head in the darkness to look at me. She then tapped her fingers on my chest.

"Go on, Monsieur. I am fascinated."

"It was the first day of school," I went on. "First grade, I mean. Not pre-school or kindergarten. We lived out in the country, so I took a bus to school. On the first day, my older sister went out to the bus stop before me. I walked out of the house to join her and saw her there with a girl my age, who was wearing a purple dress. I remember that, all these years later. A purple dress, and she was a goddess and I fell in love with her right then and there. I mean it. Love."

"Love at first sight, Elon. My goodness. I am not skeptical, but curious. Are you not sure these years later it is now some dreamlike memory?"

"I am sure all these years later I know what adult love is, and I felt that way then for this girl. I know love. I didn't know sex, I wasn't developed sexually, but I knew love. Romantic love. I fell in love again later on with another girl, when I was ten. Not puppy love, but love just as deep as I felt later on as an adult. Same as for the girl in the purple dress in the first grade. It always bothered me to hear about puppy love. That was demeaning for how I felt. I've had crushes, too. I know what a crush is, but I know and knew the full extent of love, back then."

She leaned over and kissed me on the cheek.

"Back to the first grade," I continued. "I was quickly teacher's pet and talked my teacher into letting me sit next to this girl. My teacher just thought that was adorable and let me do it, sit next to her. And I sat with this girl on the bus every day going to school and coming from school. I'd spend lunch breaks with her while we were at school during the day, and we'd walk around the school grounds holding hands. It embarrassed my sister, and she told our mother. But my mother loved it. I was just the cutest little boy to her. Then one day I asked if I could have this girl over to spend the night with me. My mother actually called her mother and arranged it. That seemed natural to me and something a mother should do for her adorable son."

"Oh, Elon," Brigitte said, laughing. Her taps on my chest were forceful. "Your mother surely did not arrange for you to spend the night with your little school sweetheart. And surely her mother did not agree to this. My God. This is marvelous."

"It was arranged," I assured. "The very next Friday night, her mother drove her over to our house to spend the night. My sister helped her wash her hair and put it in rollers. We had supper, watched television, and played jacks. That's a girl's game back home. Maybe you know of it. Then it was time for bed. But instead of sleeping with me, she goes and sleeps in my sister's room. I couldn't believe it and protested. Somehow I was supposed to understand that she should sleep with my sister instead of me. But I did not understand in the least. This is not spending the night together at all, and I was bugged about it. This is her coming over and sleeping with my sister after a family time together. I had no idea about sex, of course. Didn't even cross my mind, but I knew I wanted her next to me."

"Oh, Elon, this is wonderful. What a story. My God. But all the more, Elon, why would someone like you not already be married?"

"I don't know, Brigitte. I loved girls later on, enough to marry. But college, the Marines, then travel... All this was my destiny somehow."

I turned to her shadowy figure.

"Why not you?" I asked her. "You also were no virgin when we met."

"I fell in love once," she answered. "Very deeply. While still in school back home. Before I went to the university. He was a car mechanic. A very nice fellow. Hard working, very good-looking and muscular. A man's man. The strong-and-silent type. He was very good to me and showed me much respect. When I went to college I still loved him, but after a year at the university I needed more from him. He was smart, but not in a book way. I wasn't satisfied anymore with him, though the hormones were still there. It was just hormonal, I suppose, now that I look back. A young girl developing her hormones. He introduced me to the sexual world. I am grateful to him for that. There were things to admire about him, but he began to seem dull. The university opened up so much in me. That is why I was glad to come here. I wanted more in my life, suddenly. The university gave me ideas I wanted to live out."

"It makes you believe all the more in the cosmos and us, doesn't it, Brigitte?"

"I suppose this is why I am so possessive about you. The first time I really loved someone. Beyond the hormones. Soul-to-soul love."

"Soul-to-soul love," I concurred.

"I believe in us," she said with emotion. She laid her head on my shoulder. "How we were meant to be. I feel our destiny."

Chapter 19

"Remember those propaganda pieces before a movie here," I said as I looked up from my American newspaper. "Well, maybe they weren't just propaganda. I'm reading here that Taiwan is leaving the mainland far behind in production and wealth per capita. Like Taiwan gets it and Chairman Mao didn't, when he was alive."

"What are you talking about?" Brigitte asked from the chair opposite me.

"You know, while we're waiting for the movie to start we'd see these video clips on the screen there in the movie theater that showed brilliant light coming from the small Taiwan island and lighting up the vast mainland."

"Yes, I remember them coming on before these little one-hour movies that were two hours long in Hollywood. I still don't know what 'The Deer Hunter' was about. It was the worst experience of my life to see a Hollywood movie here. So edited and cut up it was little more than highlights. That's why we don't go anymore."

"I know, but I'm not talking about the movie. You're on another subject. Before the movie they had advertisements, but also propaganda. That. The propaganda stuff."

"Okay, I get it," she said. "Yes, Taiwan needs to

142

feel important, so they make propaganda for themselves. But you're right. I agree with them. They have figured it out. They are years ahead of the mainland, economically and politically. Freedom and wealth created here. So I am for them. They can have their propaganda. Hooray for them."

"We're on the same page finally," I said, feeling gratified.

"What are you getting at, Elon, my boy?"

"I've been reading the news. Now with Mao gone, there are reformers in charge. It's still the Communist Party, but there is a power struggle these days. Old guard versus reformers. Remember, we talked about this before. Deng is the key reformer now and has most of the power. A lot of the reformers were persecuted by Mao. Mao wasn't working out well, overall. No freedoms, no wealth, just a controlled population. Hippies liked him more than the Chinese did. The people were tired of working sixteen-hour days on a commune and not being allowed to keep much for themselves. I know I'm oversimplifying."

"Yes, you oversimplify. But there is occult worship in China of Mao by some."

"I know. It's more complicated than I stated. But a lot were tired of him, too. Anyway, there were guys in the party giving Mao a hard time, and he denounced and vilified them. Now that he's dead, in the new power struggle, free market ideas are coming out. It looks like some of this might take hold. They may start emulating Taiwan at least more in their economy, though not government."

I looked at her for emphasis.

"This is exciting," I said with a smile. "Right here

in our own back yard."

"I wonder what that means for Taiwan," Brigitte mused. "If the free market takes form on the mainland someday, will Taiwan be satisfied to reunite with them? I would think not, since it's still the same government there on the mainland. But at least they wouldn't be starving if the mainland took over. They could keep their free market system, I suppose."

"You know they would hate being stuck with these dictators," I said. "It's still the Communist Party in charge, free market oriented or not. The political structure is still the old one and probably has to be, to implement all these reforms. While they are reforming a hundred eighty degrees economically, the people don't know what's going on and probably feel insecure. At least most of them."

"You like this stuff, don't you, Elon? Politics and world events and such."

"Yeah. I love it, in fact. It excites me. The real world out there. But also right next door. I could be reading this in newspapers back home, I know. But it's happening right here, and Taiwan, Korea, Japan, Hong Kong, Singapore—they're all nearby and a part of it. Interacting with it. It's better to be living some of it here, and reading about it, too, while doing so, than reading it from my sandbox back home. I get goose bumps seeing some of it first hand, not just picturing it."

She nodded in agreement.

"That's why we're here, babes," she said. "Yes, this is exciting."

She looked at me point blank.

"It's time to get your visa," she commanded. "This

is an exciting place at an exciting time. Just like you said. I don't want to leave. So while we're on the subject and you're excited about being a part of it all, hey, visa time, baby."

"I enrolled already in my new Mandarin course. I'll get my visa from it in the first couple of days after class starts."

"I'm just checking. I know we talked about it." She looked quickly at her watch. "Listen, let's take our walk to the park nearby. I want to practice Tai Chi before I get tired or hungry. It's midmorning, and people are already there by now, practicing."

"That stuff bores me," I whined.

"No, no, Elon. You are not allowed to be so bored. It's their national sport. I know it is technically a martial art more than a sport. It is good exercise and good for self-defense. I like doing it with you. We should go."

"I get plenty of exercise already."

"This is different. This will not take long. I enjoy being part of it while I am here. It is a way to be with the natives naturally, in their environment. And it is in the park. Quit giving me a hard time about this, you whiner."

I made a pronounced and pained movement as I got up from the chair. I knew she was right, but I still found Tai Chi boring. My whining at least made sure we didn't dwell on the Tai Chi movements longer than necessary.

Every hour of the day, it seemed, you could go by a park and there would be scores of people meticulously and patiently going through their movements and routines, one person dutifully instructing another if a novice wasn't sure of themselves.

The first moves of the series I had down fairly well now, as did Brigitte. She was further along, however. I admired how she loved Tai Chi, but I dwelled on what I already knew, in rebellion, to keep from having to learn more.

"I don't see why they call these moves natural," I mentioned critically as we walked back to our apartment. "It isn't natural to stand on one foot with our arms all spread out like a crane. Maybe for a crane it is, but not for me."

"You prefer to punch someone," she said with a laugh.

"I didn't have to be trained to do that, for sure. Punching is what is natural for a human. You can fine tune your punch, but I had to learn to be a crane from scratch while doing Tai Chi."

"Oh, shush," she teased me. "I like knowing I can defend myself. This is more for women anyway, but good for everyone. I like doing it with you. Even if you whine. Be my companion, please."

"I love being your companion, Brigitte. And I'll be glad someday of my memories doing Tai Chi in a park in Taipei. So let me whine a bit, and I'll be okay."

Such endeavors with Brigitte in our spare time broke up my daily routine. I was grateful for that and for sharing a joy of hers. I felt I owed her such moments. And it reassured Brigitte concerning us while I continued my encounters with Jean. For Jean was still in our lives.

"I would like to show you Sun Moon Lake, Elon," Jean said during class. "It is a major place for tourists here."

"I've seen it already," I answered her.

She looked at me painfully.

"When did you see this place, Elon? You have no car."

I considered telling her. But now that I had my new visa, I felt I should keep her as a client longer. Before the inevitable showdown.

"I took a bus," I lied.

"Oh, no, Elon. That is not the way. I can show you around."

I thought for a moment. Sun Moon Lake at least was not far away, and with a car we could see the hotspots in a day and be back to Taipei without spending the night.

"Okay," I replied. "That would be nice. You could show me places I missed."

"Oh, yes, Elon. That is certain. I could show you very beautiful places there."

I dreaded telling Brigitte. I waited until the next day while we walked from the park after doing our Tai Chi.

"Okay," Brigitte answered calmly. "See, I'm not being possessive. I am handling this well. Yes, that is probably a good plan. It is not far away, and you and I have already seen much of it. You can shuffle her through and come home."

I actually survived. This pleasantly surprised me.

"Did you take a boat ride across the lake?" Jean asked me upon our arrival that next Saturday.

I shook my head no.

"We can do that," she suggested. "A boat ride is very nice. Very peaceful. I would like to share this with you."

I let Jean handle everything. In fact, I loved being taken care of.

"Here the boat gets off at the Ita Thao Pier," she instructed while getting up from her seat to depart the boat. "We will enjoy."

As we left the pier, she turned to explain.

"This village is much as the early people in Taiwan lived."

"The aboriginal people?" I asked her.

"What you say?"

"The original inhabitants. The earliest people of an area are termed aboriginals."

"Aboriginals," she repeated. "I thought aboriginals were in Australia."

"Technically, though, they are the original inhabitants of any place."

"See, Elon, that is an English lesson for me while we enjoy our trip. Very good."

She then pointed straight ahead of us.

"Look, there is a nice temple to see. Or perhaps it is best to have tea in a restaurant near it."

"Tea is fine. I've seen plenty of temples. Let's just absorb the atmosphere."

"What is 'absorb the atmosphere'?" she asked.

"Looking at a temple gives a nice feeling," I explained. "We feel fresh, like breathing air. To enjoy the view and feel the imagery is like absorbing the surroundings."

"Yes, perhaps. Even more English lessons. We should do this instead of class."

In spite of the uniqueness of the village, Ita Thao was very much a tourist place. There was shop after shop and restaurant after restaurant, including an abundance of street vendors. We walked until we found an open-air restaurant.

Jean seemed nervous and ill at ease as we sipped our tea. She kept staring behind me, so I turned around. A young man glared unashamedly at her. I wanted to ignore him, but Jean was truly unhappy. I got up from my chair.

"No, Elon," she said. "It is nothing. Leave him be."

"Do you have a problem?" I asked him in a rough Texan voice. "You are annoying my friend."

"She is very pretty," he replied.

"I know, but that doesn't mean you can stare."

"Why is she with you? Why is she with an American? The Taiwanese are not good enough for her? She is very pretty. So tell me, she needs a Hollywood?"

"Don't worry about it. Quit staring."

He looked at me menacingly.

"I do not like you," he said.

"Who cares who you like? Quit staring at my friend."

"You are John Wayne?"

"I'm a friend of hers. Quit staring."

He looked angrily at me for a moment, then began to relax.

"I am sorry," he finally said. "I am lonely. I had a girl friend. I miss her. Then I see such a pretty girl with a Hollywood. But I had no right to make a problem. Thank you for taking up for her."

He reached up to shake my hand. I wondered if it was a trick, but reached out.

"That's all right," I said back to him as we let go our handshake. "I've been lonely too. You have a great

149

country here. Very nice people. Including you."

He smiled at me, then looked to the side as if making peace.

"I am glad you did not fight him," Jean said approvingly as I returned to our table. "You are very brave. You are a Marine. Is that not so?"

"But I would have helped you anyway," I answered.

"Elon, please, let me get you an apartment. I want to know you so much more. You are my best friend. We can have happy times. And I love America."

I could feel how much I liked her. If there was no Brigitte in my life I knew I still wouldn't want to get involved with anyone. But I would be interested in Jean.

I had to do better than this, I scolded myself. But I knew I wouldn't. This was just a test, and if there was a destiny, I had to pass. I was getting ready to hurt Jean, and I didn't want to. Maybe I would even hurt Brigitte if I didn't straighten things out.

Chapter 20

"Elon," I heard Brigitte's anxious voice say behind me.

I turned from my table to see her walk briskly my way. Was it good news or bad?

"Elon," she repeated as she sat beside me while putting her hand over mine. "I can't believe what has happened. I don't mean to make this so big, but it caught me by surprise. I talked to the owner of the folk house just now. He wanted to speak with us for three days but didn't know how to reach us. Good news. Last week there was a radio man here. A local disc jockey for a Taipei radio station show. Mostly music, but he has guest performers. He wants you. He checked you out here. Someone told him about a Texas man who sings. He really liked you but had to see about putting you on his show. Since he didn't know how to reach us except for here, he booked you in faith for tonight, right after your performance here. The owner called him just now to verify you are here and that you will appear. I know how to get to this radio station. We will go in my car in two hours, right after the show. He will interview you for a few minutes and then let you sing a song. Just you and the guitar. I will go and get your guitar now, while you are performing here."

She seemed ready to come out of her skin. Just as she got up to leave, she sat back down to talk more.

"Listen," she continued. "I know what song you should sing. The show is in Mandarin, but he will speak with you in English, of course. Fifteen minutes. An interview and a song. It is not like the BBC, and I don't mean to make this such a thing. But from nowhere, *pow*, here we are. More crumbs for us. Soon we can build a cake. Anyway, mention you are from Texas. Texas sells. Do not overbill, but casually mention it. Then sing the song 'When My Blue Moon Turns To Gold Again.' Is that the name? But sometimes you start like a ballad when you sing it. Like Bill Monroe, you told me once as you practiced in our apartment. Leave that out, the slow ballad version. Do it more like Elvis, with energy and a beat. But not so strong as Elvis. As much like Merle Haggard. In between Elvis and Merle Haggard, I mean. Remember how you explained all this to me with this song, and so many other songs, too, as you practice? See, I pay attention. I am your manager. This will work. Trust me. Be sure to include this song tonight here as a practice for when we go to the radio station. I must leave now to get your guitar."

She leaned over to kiss me in celebration, then dashed off.

Brigitte's stint as manager for the modeling agency gave her experience and confidence in her ability. She was intuitive. But now, as my manager, she was inspired, and her inspiration excited me just as much as getting to sing excited me.

"This is just another performance," Brigitte instructed as we drove to the radio station later that night. "You were nervous your first time to perform publicly. You are nervous every time before a performance, in fact. This is just another. Just another audience. You know the song, and you know your ability."

She looked quickly at me and gave a nod of assurance, then held my hand.

I was indeed nervous as I walked into the studio. But I had seen movies of singers on radio or television. I pictured myself as a star as I sat next to the DJ. This calmed me.

"And now, for English speakers in our audience," he introduced, "we have a Texas cowboy in the studio."

He looked at me then, to include me as part of the show.

"Elon, I must talk first in Mandarin to explain that for the next fifteen minutes we will be talking with you in English, so those who do not speak English should stay tuned to the show. They will enjoy you, especially with the song you prepared especially for our show."

The DJ then went into his Mandarin discourse.

"Thank you for being patient, Elon," he said after a couple of minutes.

"Thank you for having me on," I replied.

"The name Elon sounds like Elvis somehow. And you sing like Elvis, also. I have listened to you."

I laughed from embarrassment. I hated hype but hoped it worked.

"I have a different style," I said.

"If your English is good enough out there in radioland, you will notice his Texas cowboy drawl. Yes, Elon is from Texas. Just like Kenny Rogers. You sound just like Kenny Rogers."

How could I sound like Kenny Rogers *and* like Elvis? I wondered.

"Thank you," I said shyly. "I don't really sound

like anyone."

"How modest of you. So, Elon, are you a cowboy? We hear so much about cowboys and Texas. Where is your hat?"

"I left it back home. Yes, I'm a cowboy. We farm, but we also had cattle. I grew up in a rural place. Most of us were cowboys."

"You left your horse in Texas, it seems."

He was beginning to sound like Joe Cool to me.

"Yes, I did. And our pickup truck. I don't need them here in Taipei."

"What brings you here, Elon? How did a Texas cowboy find his way to Taiwan without his horse? We are thrilled to have you."

"After I got out of the Marines, I wanted to see the world."

"So you were in the Marines. Did you go to Vietnam? Were you in the Marines during the war?"

"Yes, I was. And also Okinawa. That's not far from here. I love the Far East and always wanted to see more. Taiwan appealed to me, and I heard I could teach English here. So I came to check it out."

"Very nice. We are so glad you did. So you teach English?"

"Yes, I teach at the English Language Institute. A Mr. Chu and his wife run the school, and I have very intelligent students. I am very impressed with Taiwan. I'm very glad I'm here. The Far East is very exotic to me."

"Well, you got in a praise for your school. They will be happy to hear. Perhaps more students will come to you now."

"It's a great school. I hope more come. I would

love that. Look me up if you do."

"We hear so much about the Marines, Elon. You are a tall Texan, and also a Marine. For our radio friends, he is tall, blond, and muscular. A true cowboy, just like in the movies. With a great voice, just like in the movies. So, Elon, that brings us to why you are here—to show our audience what a singing cowboy sounds like in person, right here on our radio show. What will you sing? You brought your guitar. We are waiting to hear from you."

"This is a bluegrass song. I know bluegrass is from Kentucky, but I will sing a Texas arrangement of it. It's called 'When My Blue Moon Turns to Gold Again.'"

"Excellent. Wonderful, Elon. Please do so."

I was self-conscious as I picked up my guitar. Despite all the times I had sung publicly, including for two hours just prior to this interview, my nervousness returned full force as I pictured all the people listening on their radios to hear me. I concentrated on Brigitte. I pictured her, knowing she listened in her car.

Once I strummed the guitar, however, and began the song, the nervous energy turned to confidence. I belonged here.

Brigitte beamed at me the entire drive back to our apartment. I was her man. Not her product, but her man.

"Elon, you were not a singer before you came to Taiwan. Not professionally, anyway. But when your moment came in the folk house that night when you sang, your audition, you were like a master. How, my love? How? Who are you that this happened?"

Her adulation embarrassed me. I looked at her to explain.

"I told you that already," I said, self-conscious

155

again. "I was shy and had little confidence, but through the years I came to terms with a dream I always had. Then you."

"I don't want you to repeat what you said before. Tell me more. All this is happening now, and I cannot believe I am seeing all this and all you have to say is that I inspired you and now this."

"My father sang in church when I was growing up. Solos, I mean. It made me think I could too. But when I was told to sing solo one day in school, at a young age, I was horrible because I was so nervous. Gasping for breath from shyness. And later, when I bought a cassette player, I sang into the microphone and it sounded terrible. Like a drone. I couldn't live with that. I had serious doubts about myself, like I talked about before. There was a struggle to overcome the doubts. The worry about being just another Joe Cool. But the dream wouldn't leave me. I'd listen to the radio and want to be like the singers I heard. Finally, the dream overcame the doubts. Especially when I heard Hank Williams, a singer and song writer that lived his songs, deep, soulful songs. I kept singing to myself and releasing my own Hank Williams inside."

"He is this man that wrote that song you sing," she broke in. "This gospel song you sing every show. The 'walking for the Lord' song."

I nodded yes.

"So I couldn't live with myself and not do that, somehow. What Hank did. And Patsy Cline singing 'Crazy' inspired me just as much. I sang 'Crazy' in the car, or walking on the sidewalk, probably in my sleep. Imitating her, then letting out my own special feelings, too, as I did so. I had to find a way to be good."

I shrugged, not knowing what else to say.

"You know," I said with another shrug, "it all came together when I came to Taiwan and met you. Let me say it. I want to say it again and again because it is true."

"Your manager," she said with a laugh. "You can tell me that again. I love hearing this."

"My manager," I said appreciatively. "Mine. Only mine. And the one I had to be a somebody for or die."

She squeezed my hand. I was glad she'd brought it up again. I needed to share these things with her.

As I rode my bicycle the next morning to the school, I hoped my students had heard me on the radio. My hope was as much to embellish the school as about me and what they didn't know until now.

"Mr. Chu," some of my class said excitedly at the school. "Did you hear Elon last night on the radio? The Charlie Ming show? Did you hear him? He mentioned our school. He has made you famous, Mr. Chu. Our school is famous."

Mr. Chu nodded that he'd heard the show and looked appreciatively my way. Maybe I could drop Jean soon and be forgiven.

All of my classes ignored the lessons from our book while we spoke of my performance on the radio. I wasn't bored, for once.

Then, like clockwork, the cosmos reappeared.

"My papa wrote me," Brigitte said as she looked up from a letter. "There is no hurry, he told me now. Since I am happy in Taiwan, it is fine for me to stay longer. But he assumes I will be coming home someday not so long from now. Why would I want to stay here, he seems to think, half way around the world in a poor country. It is of no mind that I have a good and happy job. He cannot see this as possible to be happy. Just an experience. Then someday I grow up and return."

"He wants you to take over the farm somehow," I surmised.

She nodded yes.

"He mentioned this. And there is this boy I grew up with that works with cars. The one I told you about when we were talking about our past romances. This one. The mechanic. This man asks about me. My father has ideas. He is just talking now, but he has ideas."

"Do you feel obliged to take over the farm?" I asked, seeing where this was leading. "Some sort of emotion or pressure?"

"It is a pressure," she answered. "Some sentiment also. My sister is now living a different life. She does not want to farm. I have pity on my father. This farm has been in our family since before his grandparents, since last century, maybe more. I don't know how far back. It was bigger once, but other ancestor siblings along the way took some. Some of the land came back if a sibling family didn't farm it. We rent some and bought some back. It is still a small farm compared to America, but profitable with all the subsidies to protect agriculture security in Europe. From all the wars before. To take it over does have an appeal. And my life perspectives have changed now because of you."

She looked at me quizzically.

"There is no hurry, Elon. But if we marry and you miss your old farm, would you be happy in Europe with me?"

I nodded my head approvingly.

"I worked on a dairy farm one summer in Bavaria,"

I commented. "Before I began my trek across Asia. I very much enjoyed it. Even though the farms are smaller in Europe than ours back home, it was still hard work. And I loved living in Europe."

She smiled at my answer.

"We can get married here, right?" I asked, as if to answer yes to her notion.

"Do you want to wait until just before we go back, or should we do it now?" she inquired. "It matters not to me either way. I am happy with our arrangement as it is."

"You would have to give up the modeling agency," I mused. "If we went to your home. Our home-to-be. You're happy here. And I may be on the verge of better things in singing here. It is tempting to stay, but tempting to take over your father's farm. So let's look into getting married here. But also, let's adjust to all of this going on. Decide if you do want to go back to take over the farm, and if so, when."

"I am sure I want to go back," she answered without hesitation. "I am sure of it. I like very much the idea of farming in my home with you. Raising a family in our village. Until now, this idea seemed such a tedious thought. But suddenly I find it very appealing. Yes, let us take time to think this over and adjust. But I can tell you, it is what I want."

Chapter 21

"Somebody stole my bicycle," I complained as I arrived home from work. "It was a good bike, too. I love bicycles, and it was a good bike that I got cheap. Now I have to walk to work. That adds a half hour each way."

"Can you not get another bicycle, Elon?" Brigitte asked sympathetically.

"How much longer are we going to be here?"

"Get a cheap one, mon ami. Then you can throw it away whenever we leave."

"I'll take a bus from now on. It just irks me. And to be stolen from. It's like I've been violated. Someone feels superior to me. He got me, or something."

"Yes, it is not a good feeling. Take a bus. But better is to buy a cheap bicycle."

"It sounds like we're staying longer," I mused. "I don't mind. You seem happy."

"Yes, I am happy here. You and I will be together no matter when we leave. And when we leave, we will be in Belgium forever. So while I am here, I do love my life. As long as our mischievous Greek gods allow, we will stay longer."

It had more to do with Jean than the gods, I was sure.

"Elon," Jean said to me abruptly as I tried getting her to read from the text in our class. "I made a reservation in a resort in Kenting Town for the next weekend for the two of us. Not this weekend coming now, but for the next weekend. Friday night and Saturday night. I want to show you this lovely place on the most southern tip of Taiwan at this wonderful resort. We talked about this before. I wish to do so now."

"I was going to fly to Okinawa next weekend," I lied. "I used to be stationed there in the Marines. I wanted to revisit since I now live so close."

"Oh, no, Elon. Please not. Come with me. Please. I have planned. I want so much to show you and share."

"Let me see if I can get a refund for my ticket, if I can cancel the reservation. But I was supposed to meet a friend of mine from those days there. For old times."

"I will pay for the refund if you can not get it from cancelling. Your friend can meet you the next weekend perhaps. Please, Elon."

I felt so gutless. This was the perfect setting to let her know of my status with Brigitte. But I couldn't make myself do it.

"You mean this entire time," Brigitte groaned, "this girl Jean has stayed attracted to you. You never talk about her anymore. I almost forgot about her, with all the excitement of us getting married. But she still wants to shack up with you. It was bad enough about the apartment she wanted, but now a sex holiday at a resort?"

"She has behaved herself," I replied. "More than I thought she would. So I didn't speak much about her so as to not cause any problems. She does remind me of her desires sometimes, though, like now. I turn her down and she is good about it. But no denying it, she still wants me."

"How cozy. How marvelous all this."

I looked at Brigitte nervously.

"I'm not being possessive here, Elon. This is disgust. I feel huge disgust."

"She took me to Sun Moon Lake. I don't know if I told you."

"Yes, you told me that. But that was three weeks ago."

"You trust me, and I won't cheat on you. I'm not going with her to Kenting Town. I just was trying to be honest with you because it is a dramatic leap. The leap we feared."

She nodded with a jerk of her head.

"I can handle this," she said as if reassuring herself while turning to look away. She let out a sigh. "I feel secure about us. I don't feel possessive now. But it is still to wrestle with, concerning this Jean girl and her wanting you."

She looked at me again and eased into a smile.

"Maybe I am too possessive still, a bit. Sorry, Elon. But I believe you love me and want to marry me and have tried with this Jean girl, and you are loyal to your boss, Mr. Chu. It all is complicated and part of survival, too, in a way. But don't tell me any more about her. Let us not tempt fate. But Elon, this is more deep about her, this weekend she wants with you. I understand why you had to tell me. Yes, she has been behaving, like you say, but still she is waiting for you to open up to her. It sounds like her patience is running out and the push is on for you. She hasn't quit hoping. I even feel some pity for her, since she doesn't know about me. She is not trying to cause mischief. It is a luxury for me to take pity on her, but I must say, I do have some pity."

Brigitte looked at me intensely as if contemplating something.

"We must solve all this now, Elon."

"Is this our cue to marry now?" I asked.

"I think this pushes us, yes, but we were going to do that anyway."

"I'll tell Mr. Chu at the school. He knew I was going to leave eventually. Not so far away, but soon. So. And he has more students now because of me, with the mention of his school on the radio. He is grateful to me for that."

"Each time," Brigitte said while looking at me affectionately, "some event, usually about this Jean girl, makes another catalyst. She is a chemical agent in our lives, it seems. There is always some catalyst in our situations."

"I guess I can handle you thinking of her as a catalyst," I said to lighten things. "You used to think worse about her."

"I will look tomorrow with what we must do to marry," she continued. "The easiest way to do so. We must do so now. Marry now. As soon as we can arrange. I will tell my parents. You must also tell yours, but mine especially we must inform that we intend to come and farm. My father must know that when he retires, we will support him and my mother. That will make him happy. Maybe we should invite Jean to the wedding. That is a sad joke, to make sure you understand. But you must agree, she has been a marvelous catalyst on our behalf. Yes, let us be glad she is but a catalyst."

Chapter 22

Brigitte looked up from her letter.

"I did not tell my parents yet we are to marry. I have not written them about this. I wanted to arrange our marriage first, to be sure when and to know if there is some unexpected difficulty that troubles our doing so."

I waited for more as she paused to think.

"There is yet another catalyst in our life now, Elon. I do not know whether to be amazed or annoyed. It is getting to where I want all these catalysts out of my life."

She looked at me apologetically.

"Our lives, I mean," she emphasized. "All these catalysts that keep coming."

She shook her head in frustration.

"*Merde!*" she exclaimed. "*Merde, merde, merde.* I must call my father. Do not be alarmed. I still want to farm with him."

She walked toward the telephone, then turned back toward me as if to answer my confusion.

"My father wants me to come home and take over the farm. No more thinking about it or hinting, that is what he wants. He just told me absolutely. He is very insecure now that he is getting older and soon not to be able to farm so much physically. He needs a man to help. I can run the farm as well as a man once I learn everything. But some things are so physical it would be difficult for me. Plus I would need to raise children someday. So I must tell you. This car mechanic that lives in our village near our farm keeps asking about me. He sees a farm in the arrangement, I am sure. He is a nice man, and I am sure he would like to marry anyway. I am available, he thinks, since I live half way around the world temporarily and have a farm in my portfolio. I don't blame this man or my father. I understand how both of them are seeing a hopeful situation, but I find it very intruding. I think I would consider marrying him except for you, but I have a life to live too."

She began to shake her head again.

"This is worse than Jean," she bit out. "Everywhere a catalyst."

"But Jean is here," I noted. "You at least only get letters about your catalyst."

"I am not so sure I just spoke the truth," she continued, oblivious to anything I had said. "Even on a farm I want more from life than I would have with this mechanic man. He would be good on the farm, but I need more from my husband. For my sanity."

She looked at me.

"I need you," she emphasized.

She thought more and shook her head yet again.

"This cosmos thing in our lives," she groaned. "Can it not see how we were going to get married even without my father and without Jean? Perhaps our cosmos is confused about us, since we drag our feet. We both were very independent in our lifestyle. So the cosmos is nervous, I suppose. Hard to convince. Many people fall in love, then change their plans. We would have gotten married anyway, I am sure. This cosmos thing, however, keeps putting nails in our coffin. Maybe that is not a good way to say things."

"I would have chosen a better example," I said with a laugh, "but I get what you're talking about. Yeah, God, or whoever—time out. You got our attention."

She walked over to kiss me, then eased into a smile.

"I am tired of talking about the cosmos," she said. "I do not believe this, after all. That is too simple. We did this. Not Jean, not my father, not some mechanic. We did all this about us. *Voilà*. Okay. That settles it. We want to get married. We want this soon. We are doing so. Now, even sooner. So that settles that."

She walked briskly to the telephone.

"I must call my father," she said. "I must tell him, now, about us and our plans. It will be midmorning in Belgium. He may be out, but perhaps my mother is in the house. Perhaps it is best I talk with her anyway, as a mediator in this. Anyway, you and I are getting married. They will understand. It is their duty as a catalyst, even. Ha."

I listened as Brigitte talked on the telephone. Eventually, she looked at me.

"Would you like to talk to my mother?" she asked me. "She speaks only French. Just say hello."

I shook my head no. A few minutes more conversation and Brigitte hung up.

"They are thrilled," she said exuberantly. "Or at least my mother is. She will tell Papa at lunch. He is in town now. She assured me he would be accepting. I would think a farm boy from Texas is better to take over the farm than a car mechanic, even if a Belgian one. They will be happy about us."

I nodded approval.

"So," she huffed, "it is set, then. I want to marry today. I am excited, Elon. I have registered us already and shown all our documents. It is now just for them to approve the procedure. The formality. So by tomorrow I think they are ready for us to marry legally. I hope we don't need another catalyst. We are ready to marry now, God, or whoever. No more thinking or prodding needed. Here we go. We are ready now. Today or as soon as we can be allowed. Get it? This is us, me and Elon, getting married now. Okay, God?"

She winked.

"Should we take our honeymoon while we're waiting?" I asked as a joke.

"Where are we going for this honeymoon?"

"We talked already about Kenting Town."

"But Jean was going to take you there. It is used already."

"She took me to Sun Moon Lake, too. This is a small country. Kenting Town sounds like the best honeymoon spot. A beach, a nice resort, lakes around, small ones anyway. Forests. A nice area and all the way down to the southern point of the country."

"Yes, I want this," she said thoughtfully. "I just feel sad for Jean. I don't know why. It seems cheating her. But such is life."

"You don't feel sorry for her," I chided. "Nice try, though."

"I know I don't," she replied. "Perhaps a little. Enough to fool the gods, I hope. But listen, Elon, no more hesitating. I am going to find this justice of the peace here. No more waiting. Come with me. What if now is good?"

I had no idea where we were as Brigitte drove us. She was pure business on the drive and after we arrived. She did not wait on me upon arrival. It was up to me to keep up with her.

"I now pronounce you man and wife," the JP said, just like back in America.

"Congratulations," the two borrowed witnesses said after Brigitte and I kissed to make the formality complete.

"We did it," Brigitte said with a gleam.

I kissed her again for an encore.

"I suddenly feel married," I commented. "I'm shocked, in a way. Just an hour ago we were still waiting to find out when we could. Suddenly, *pow*, here we are. I love it. I'm married to you. It feels marvelous. Just like that. Let's go home and tell our parents."

"It's like a magic wand," Brigitte said happily. "I do feel married. It was just to be a formality, but I'm the happiest I've ever been. I love you, Elon."

Our arms locked in embrace all the way back home.

"My parents want to meet you," I told Brigitte after talking on the phone with them about my marriage. "Let's spend our honeymoon there. In America."

"I would like to see America. Even Texas, if that is the only place we go. But no. We met here, we married here. Kenting Town is where we will spend our honeymoon. And this weekend there is a Buddhist festival there. There will be parades and so much food. I mean more food than before, at a normal time. Festival occasion food."

"We need to leave Taiwan right afterwards, Brigitte. I still haven't told Mr. Chu about you. Only my modeling agency—ha, meaning you. But not the English school."

"Or your Jean."

"Or her. Or the folk house. I need to do all this now that we're legal and married. Let's don't wait on another catalyst, because for sure there is one coming any second."

"I am sure of that," Brigitte said with a giggle. "We can set our watches to that."

"I'll tell Mr. Chu and Jean this afternoon. I have a class with her."

"I must settle with my agency," Brigitte commented deep in thought. "They must soon find a replacement."

"Tell them this afternoon," I suggested. "Tell them our honeymoon is this weekend and we hope to go to America in a week and then to settle in Belgium."

"Yes, yes, I can do that. You are right. They can manage. They have staff that know things. They know how. They will find a way."

I was nervous as I went to the school. I left early so I could prepare Mr. Chu before I told Jean.

"Brigitte and I got married this afternoon, Mr. Chu," I began. "I barely mentioned her before, but we have been serious about one another for several months now. I have been a model for her agency since my arrival here. We have pressure from back home to return. In our case it will be Belgium. We are taking over her father's farm there, and he needs us now. So…"

Mr. Chu looked at me with a serious demeanor as I

told him. A week wasn't much for him to rearrange classes among other instructors while seeking a new instructor to replace me. But he'd had to deal with such situations before. I was very glad I had promoted him on the radio. It helped ease my conscience.

So now, Jean.

She gave a heavy, depressed sigh as I detailed my story. The best lie I could derive in my still gutless way. I kept talking without pause, to make sure I got it all out before any possible confrontation.

"I will be leaving after next week, Jean. My father wants me to farm with him and I told him I would."

"But you said he lost the farm."

"He still custom farms," I explained to continue my lie. "That's when you use your equipment, things like harvesters and planters and such, and hire them out with yourself as the driver. It can be a nice living. He has been doing that and now wants to expand his operations and needs my help."

"So you would live in Texas?"

"In a very remote farming area. There isn't much to do there besides work, which is fine with me since I'll be doing so much farming."

"So this is good-bye. You are telling me good-bye."

"Yes. Thank you for all you've shown me, Jean."

She said no more, politely smiled, handed me her class book, and walked away.

Chapter 23

"After living in sin for nearly half a year," Brigitte said chirpily, "it's marvelous to be married now that we are on our honeymoon. Happy honeymoon, darling."

I smiled as my answer.

Even on our honeymoon it seemed the great cosmos was involved, however. If I had gone with Jean before, or if our honeymoon had been at any other time, we would have missed the Buddhist festival Brigitte had mentioned in our planning stage. Now was the perfect time to be here. And here we were indeed.

"There are so many facets of Buddhism," I said as we walked along, seeing all the robed devotees in parks, pavilions, and temples. "I was interested in Buddhism as early as eight years old. The nonviolence and discipline of it appeals to Christian culture. But Buddhism is new to us in the Western world and so breaks the mold a bit. It's close enough to identify for some people, but different enough to create curiosity. I think that's the appeal."

"This festival spurred something inside you," Brigitte said playfully.

"Yeah," I replied, "this gets me deep."

"So you didn't convert to Buddhism, obviously. I was brought up Catholic. I love so much of the teaching, the instruction, and the rituals of my faith. But there is a world out there. Somewhere in that world we are on our own. We have a good foundation from our culture, but there is always a changing world."

"That's why there are monks," I added. "Both Christians and Buddhists rely a lot on monks and nuns. Specialists. They present a structure of spiritual barrier islands, to keep as much of the world away as possible. I understand the need for purity, but how can God be infinite and so structured too? Yet there is a need for things like convents and monasteries. Spiritually speaking, they are like seed banks."

"What?"

"If all you have available to plant your crops are hybrid seeds, weird things happen. Bad things happen, not just good. Not just better resistance or higher yields, or shorter or taller stalks, whatever it is you think you need. There gets to be such a variety of DNA combinations that somewhere chaos happens. Good things happen, but a lot of bad too. So you need seed banks with pure strains. If hybrids don't give you the result you want, then with the pure strains you can create your own hybrids that you know work, and then experiment more."

"My goodness, Elon, first we come to a resort on our honeymoon, then seek out a Buddhist festival, then get on to scientific farming as part of the talk about Buddhism. But such talks make our honeymoon special. We will be busy and settled on our farm, but we will talk like this sometimes. And teach our children. I would like that."

I nodded approvingly at the thought.

"You read often, Elon. Did you always, or only since you began traveling? I'm sure you read at your university studies you loved so much."

"I always loved books," I answered. "We led a practical life on the farm, and then a spiritual one in church. But books—they go so many places. My mother taught me how to read some before I started school. The more I learned to read, the more I wanted."

"It was addictive," she surmised.

"No, that's not it. It opened new worlds. It allured, not addicted. My first forms of traveling were books, you might say. I came across the stored knowledge in other cultures and histories. Ideas and knowledge are powerful. Books had all that. Traveling does, too. I had a good home but was always adventurous. I wanted more of the world even at an early age. So I would run away from home. Not from anger but for adventure. Instead of packing an extra set of clothes or some food, though, I would pack books and run away to a forest nearby. My parents didn't even know I was gone. They thought I must be out in the cow pasture with our animals or playing with my next-door neighbor. But I'd adventure to the woods and read. The trouble with that was my mother made tacos every Saturday night. That's when I would run away, on my day off, on Saturday. And I loved tacos. So I would go home for supper for the tacos."

Brigitte laughed and wrapped her arm inside of mine.

"This is the man I married," she said. "I find out more reasons why."

We walked along in our embrace and saw more of the festival. There was the fragrance of incense all around, devotees chanting, and worshippers praying. I identified with the search I saw.

"There are legends," I said as I watched the

proceedings, "that Jesus made his way to India or some such place and learned from Buddhist monks. There is an amazing amount of overlap in some of the concepts in each religion, Buddhist and Christianity."

"Tell me," she said. "I don't know so much about Buddhism."

"Both are strong believers in peace. Except that many of each religion are not up to nonviolence. Like I wasn't up to turning the other cheek. But it is there strongly in each religion. The Tibetan Buddhist monks even fought with firearms against the Chinese when the Chinese took over Tibet back in the 1950s. If a Tibetan monk falters when tested, what do the rest of us do? We are all human. We are either right for fighting in spite of what God expects, or we must keep seeking strength and wisdom until we are able to subsist without violence. I haven't given up on turning the other cheek, but I won't just memorize some passage and die a fool over it. If it is some ultimate truth, I want to be up to it. Not just be a devotee that disciplines. Or ends up a pious airhead."

"Like when the bully beat you up and you saw your own weaknesses and wanted to find this strength, which began your travels."

I nodded agreement.

"We must do better than follow or memorize," I said. "Those are the baby steps. To believe is only to lead us, not bind us."

"We must develop and mature," Brigitte concurred.

"Even everyday life in the Marines taught me about understanding life in more depth, not just following some straight and narrow path. When I was overseas, it could get very lonely. Even in the States it could, but overseas more so because of living in a new culture and missing home. When we'd get paid, so many of my buds would blow their entire paycheck in just a few days, many just going to a bar and drinking it away. The loneliness made it worse in that there would be bargirls there just to take your money. They would sit with you and talk and drink a soda or orange juice while you bought beer after beer after beer. All at inflated prices aimed at taking a sucker for everything he's worth. I would sit in the barracks and read during such times. I had a car and made two car payments a month with my small salary, plus saved money for college."

"You were smart and disciplined, Elon. Just like now."

"And judged my buddies for being fools. But one night I decided to go out with them, just to check it out. Why were they doing this irresponsible stuff? And sure enough, they were sitting and talking to a girl, buying drinks for her and themselves until the money was all gone. Craziest thing I ever saw. I felt so superior. They didn't even make a play for the girl. There were prostitutes for that. But where most of the money went wasn't for prostitutes but just to sit and talk to this girl next to them."

"This is not only crazy, Elon. I feel a pity for them as I listen to you about them. Yes, the loneliness must have been horrible."

"Yes, it was, and I was not immune to it, as I found out. I found a bar girl and began to talk, too. It felt so good just to be with a girl and talk to her. Even if you had to buy her friendship, being with her and saying something and hearing her sweet voice was good. I had to make myself not spend all night buying us drinks. I left soon and never went back. But I had to make myself not go back."

"Like turning the other cheek, you mean, Elon? This is what you are saying with your story. You weren't above it after all. Enough to discipline, but it took pushing yourself to do the wise and correct thing. You were as shallow as your friends, easily."

"Yeah, Brigitte. That's exactly right. I was not so above them after all. Just enough to be able to discipline. But I appreciated the experience. There I was judging them, and they deserved my judgment some. But also now I understood better. The experience added depth to my judgment. They seemed more human to me then, and I felt more human too, after experiencing it all."

"So here we are at this Buddhist festival, and we have scientific farming, and now being a Marine overseas as part of our sharing Buddhism. Just like the lady vendor that sold us the sausage was saying. This is true Buddhism, not just scripture and priests."

"Yeah, exactly," I replied. "There is so much overlap to religion and life. That is the purpose, even. And there is so much overlap between many religions."

"Like Christianity and Buddhism. So tell me more comparisons, Elon."

"Some Buddhists believe that works and learning are for nothing. That faith is the answer. Calling out to some Buddhist savior. That sounds like Christianity to me. Other Buddhists believe salvation is through good deeds. You know, like we hear about Judaism. Some Buddhists have believed in eternal Hell and that only the savior Buddhahood can save you from this damnation. Not all Buddhists believe these things. There are so many different aspects. It's an old religion, spread out over so many cultures and lands. Anyway, I find it all so interesting. I don't want to believe anything as much as see a vast perspective. I can't know everything, but I want to know so much more."

"We must continue to grow while we live our mundane life on the farm," she added. "Our farm life and physical survival is part of the search. But we must grow spiritually. Living day to day also is spiritual in its own way."

"Yes, that," I agreed. "Even our mundane life on the farm is knowledge and enlightenment, too. As part of the perspective. Just like we talked about when seeing the drive and hunger of the Taiwanese. Life is so beyond any religion. Religion confines as much as it enlightens. Believing religiously often causes harm and war. It's so complex. Keep searching. Don't just blindly believe."

We walked on, reveling in our thoughts as we watched the festivities. Finally, Brigitte perked up as if in some new direction.

"Back to earth," she said while looking around. "I am hungry. Let's get some exotic dish from one of these vendors or restaurants. I have no idea what these dishes are. We will just point to a dish."

We walked until we found a vendor where the aroma was intoxicating.

"What are we eating, Elon?"

"I don't want to know," I replied with a moan. "Their recipes are so good because they were poor so often and had to eat what they could get, so I've heard. They had to find a way to make even yuck foods taste good. I don't know if we are eating yuck or not. Maybe we're eating monkey brains or rat hearts. It all tastes good from the recipes, and that's all I want to know."

"Oh, you are terrible, Elon. Yes, I have heard also about these great recipes from poor areas of China. But please, your descriptions. I hope what we eat is not that bad. Anyway, you are correct, my dear. I don't want to know what we are eating either. So many food choices around. No telling what they serve. The taste is marvelous. It is good to not know what it is."

"Where do we go next?" I asked. "When we finish eating."

"Let's just drive. The scenery is as good as the food."

We drove through hills and forests along the way as we ventured back to the resort after our meal at the festival.

"Let's go to Kaohsiung," I suggested along the way, feeling adventurous. "It's the second largest city in Taiwan, and it's not far from here. It's this far south."

"I want to be here," she countered. "I love the forests. How far is Kaohsiung?"

"I don't know. We have a car. It's a narrow island. Can't be that far."

"It is their major port," she commented. "That is too working class for my mood on our honeymoon. I am sure other parts are nice, but we don't have time to find them since we don't know our way around. What can we do there that we can't do in Taipei?"

"Go to a restaurant."

"There are restaurants everywhere, and we just ate, silly boy."

"We'll have room for more food by the time we find the Modern Toilet Restaurant."

She looked at me nauseously.

"What are you talking about, crazy one?"

"One of my students told me about this restaurant in Kaohsiung called the Modern Toilet Restaurant, where the seats are old toilets. The bowls you eat from are miniature toilets. And some of the pastry is shaped like poop."

"Stop!" she shrieked. "I will take you and leave you there if you say more. My God. I want to gag. Yuck."

"Me too when I heard all this stuff," I said with a laugh. "We just had a great meal and peaceful talk. Time for some mischief."

"You hope to ruin everything," she said. "Happy honeymoon, remember. Aagh. New subject, please. We are not at our resort yet, and I want to be calm when we arrive."

"You choose the subject, then."

"Okay. So what do we do now, Elon? I'm giving you another chance with your suggestions. Make me happy with thoughts now."

"We could go to a lake and relax. I want to be at the resort now, though. The lake or whatever can wait. Let's enjoy a luxury resort for the rest of the day."

"No, I didn't mean activity. I am happy for our future but sad to leave my wonderful home of so long."

I nodded in empathy.

"They are so full of life here," Brigitte added. "I am feeling regrets we are leaving. These are special people. Survivors, like us."

"Like us," I agreed, sharing affection. "We've been

surviving with them. Even inspired by them."

"That is true. So I am ready to leave, but how does one leave such a place? Will we ever return, mi amor?"

"Probably not," I replied. "But our kids will come here and do even better than us. They will want to visit the place that created our relationship."

"If it is not taken over by the mainland," she cautioned. "Anyway, yes, maybe our children will return here for us someday."

"Now I'm more ready to leave," I said wistfully. "Just thinking of all this future. Yes, our wonderful children we will have soon. They will return here for us. What a glorious thought. We will have children soon. I love that. It makes me want to get started. We leave for Texas next week, and a couple of weeks after that we start our new life. We will farm and keep Europe free and fed. Makes me feel important."

"Yes, it is important to go back home," she said with excitement. "To farm."

"What if we had stayed on our farms and had never come here?" I mused. "A depressing thought. What would we teach our children if somehow we met and got married anyway? We didn't just meet one another here, we found so much here for us. Then we found each other. We have so much to teach our children now. It gives me shivers, Brigitte. There was a plan in our doing all this. I believe that. There is a cosmos. You decided there wasn't one, but somehow we do have this destiny. For our taking."

"We found out we want to live in Kansas after all," she said smiling.

I looked at her approvingly.

"I get it," I replied. "From *The Wizard of Oz*. But

yes, we weren't sure about our farms and our homes before. It seemed like just plain Kansas then. Now it seems part of the plan prepared for us, that we should know this about home—the depth of home waiting for us now, our fulfilling home."

A few words from the author…

I was born on October 7, 1948, in Harlingen, Texas, where I grew up and worked on a cotton farm. I graduated from Harlingen High School in 1966. I attended Texas A&M, beginning that summer. In January 1970, I dropped out to enlist in the United States Marine Corps, where I served as an enlisted man attaining the rank of Sergeant, with an honorable discharge after 3 years. I worked as a computer programmer afterwards in Houston and as a civil servant for a US Air Force Base in Frankfurt, Germany. I traveled and worked in Europe for two years, which included flying to Israel in October 1973 to aid the Jewish State in the Yom Kippor War. I was also in Greece in the summer of 1974 when the war between Greece and Turkey erupted over Cyprus. I was stuck on the Greek Island of Ios for part of that war until I managed to catch a boat to Athens just in time to watch the Greek military dictatorship fold.

I returned to Texas A&M in the Fall of 1976 to finish my Bachelor's degree in Business Management. I returned to Europe afterwards and also Israel, where I lived for almost a year. I later taught English in Taiwan before returning home to get a Master's degree in Agricultural Economics, which I received in 1982. I joined the US Peace Corps in 1984 and served for three years in the Philippines. In 1987 I began work for the Swiss government as a computer programmer until 1998.

I have worked in the IT department of Texas A&M since 1998. I have three children and am presently divorced. I am Jewish.